"I forbid you to marry this girl."

The teenager stopped at the edge of the porch and swung toward his father, who stood in the doorway. "Forbid?" the boy shouted. "You're not a father, you're a dictator. I'm eighteen, old enough to do what I want. And if I want to marry my girlfriend, I will." The boy jumped down the porch steps and ran out of sight.

Alice looked to Hayes, to his handsome features, etched with a combination of worry and despair. If she tried to talk to him now, he would most likely take his anger and frustration out on her. But his relationship with his son seemed to be out of control. And foolish or not, appreciated or not, Alice planned to offer some advice....

Dear Reader,

Welcome to Silhouette Special Edition…welcome to romance.

The lazy, hazy days and nights of August are perfect for romantic summer stories. These wonderful books are sure to take your mind off the heat but still warm your heart.

This month's THAT SPECIAL WOMAN! selection is by Rita Award-winner Cheryl Reavis. *One of Our Own* takes us to the hot plains of Northern Arizona for a tale of destiny and love, as a family comes together in the land of the Navajo.

And this month also features two exciting spin-offs from favorite authors. Erica Spindler returns with *Baby, Come Back*, her follow-up to *Baby Mine*, and Pamela Toth tells Daniel Sixkiller's story in *The Wedding Knot*—you first met Daniel in Pamela's last Silhouette Special Edition novel, *Walk Away, Joe*. And not to be missed are terrific books by Lucy Gordon, Patricia McLinn and Trisha Alexander.

I hope you enjoy this book, and the rest of the summer!

Sincerely,

Tara Gavin
Senior Editor

Please address questions and book requests to:
Silhouette Reader Service
U.S.: 3010 Walden Ave., P.O. Box 1325, Buffalo, NY 14269
Canadian: P.O. Box 609, Fort Erie, Ont. L2A 5X3

ERICA SPINDLER
BABY, COME BACK

Silhouette®

SPECIAL EDITION®

Published by Silhouette Books
America's Publisher of Contemporary Romance

For the Hoffman women: Joan, Pam and Vicki.
Thanks for the love, the support
and for making me one of your own.

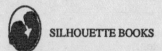 SILHOUETTE BOOKS

ISBN 0-373-09903-7

BABY, COME BACK

Copyright © 1994 by Erica Spindler

This edition published by arrangement with Harlequin Enterprises B. V.

® and TM are trademarks of Harlequin Enterprises B. V., used under
license. Trademarks indicated with ® are registered in the United States
Patent and Trademark Office, the Canadian Trade Marks Office and in
other countries.

Printed in U.S.A.

ERICA SPINDLER

believes in love at first date. Because that's all the time it took for her and her husband, Nathan, to fall in love. "We were too young. We both had to finish college. Our parents thought we should see other people, but we knew we were meant for each other," Erica says. Fourteen years later, they still know it.

Erica chose her home—Louisiana—the same way. She went "way down yonder" for a visit, fell in love with the state and decided to stay. "I may have been born in the Midwest," she says, "but I'm a true Southerner at heart."

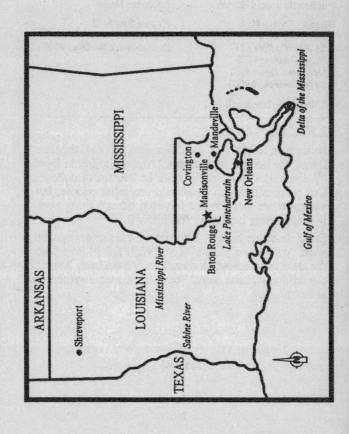

Chapter One

"Pregnant?" Alice Dougherty repeated, sucking in a sharp, surprised breath. "Are you sure?"

The teenage girl sitting across the desk from her wiped at the tears on her cheeks and nodded. "I went to the doctor."

Alice eased against her chair back and crossed her legs, working to hide her dismay and disappointment. Any overt sign of criticism and the teenager would bolt. And the fragile bond she'd struggled to form with Sheri Kane would be broken.

She cleared her throat. "How far along are you?"

The girl lifted her gaze to Alice's, then dropped it to her lap once more. She twisted her fingers together. "Nine weeks."

Seventeen years old and nine weeks pregnant. Sympathy flooded Alice. She understood Sheri's feelings only too well. She had found herself in the same position at nineteen.

Alice cleared her throat again, fighting to maintain her professional distance, to keep herself from becoming emotional. A feat she found difficult with all the kids she worked with here at Hope House, but one she found particularly difficult with Sheri. In the girl she saw too much of herself at the same age. "Have you told your father yet?"

Sheri looked up, her cheeks brightening with anger. "Oh, right. I've a got a big picture of this, me with my butt out on the street." Sheri folded her arms across her middle. "No way am I telling him!"

Alice moved her gaze over the girl, her chest tight with sympathy. Looking at Sheri Kane, the casual observer would think her the typical all-American girl next door: medium-brown hair styled in a pixie cut, big blue eyes, pretty features and a slim build. That same casual observer would assume Sheri Kane lived in a lovely home in the suburbs, that her mom baked apple pies and her nine-to-five father doted on her. Nothing could be further from the truth. Sheri's bright, pretty face masked a well of sorrow, the scars from a life of indifference and abuse.

Just another way that Sheri reminded her of herself.

Alice folded her hands in her lap. "You don't know for sure he'll kick you out."

"Oh no?" The girl jerked her chin up. "He's been telling me he would since I first got my period. 'You get yourself knocked up, girl,'" she mimicked bitterly, "'and you're out on your butt.' I figured I'd just wait until I couldn't hide the truth anymore."

And then what will you do? "Sheri, I don't think that's the best way to—"

"You're not going to change my mind," Sheri interrupted, cocking her chin a fraction more, the picture of defiance.

Alice tried another tack. "What about the baby's father? What are his feelings?"

Sheri's chin drooped, her defiance and anger evaporating like air out of a balloon. She wrung her hands. "I haven't told Jeff yet. I..." She looked at Alice, her eyes swimming with tears. "I can't. I mean, what if he hates me when he finds out? What if he's...angry? What if he—" She burst into tears and dropped her face into her hands, her shoulders shaking with the sobs.

Alice rounded the desk and put her arms around the girl. "It's okay, sweetie. We'll work through this. We will. And everything will be okay."

"I don't think so. I don't think anything will ever be...okay again."

"Oh, Sheri..." Alice stroked her hair. "I know it feels hopeless now, but these things have a way of working out. Trust me."

Sheri didn't respond, and Alice continued to stroke her hair and murmur sounds of comfort. After a time, the girl's sobs abated, becoming soft mewls of despair. The hopeless sounds pulled at Alice's heartstrings even more than the racking sobs had, and she held her a bit tighter.

When Sheri grew quiet, her breathing, finally, only slightly ragged, Alice dropped her arms and eased away. She tipped the girl's face up to hers and smiled reassuringly. "Feel a little better now?"

Sheri's eyes filled again. "Not really," she whispered, hiccuping.

Alice's heart went out to her as she saw the girl fight the tears spilling over. Sheri Kane was made of tough stuff.

Alice reached for the box of tissues she kept on her desk and handed it to the girl. Sheri took it, selected a tissue and pressed it to her eyes.

"I've messed up everything. As usual." She drew in a shuddering breath. "I feel so dumb. So stupid and useless."

Those were Sheri's parents' words. Their thoughts. Just as they had been her own parents'. Anger surged through Alice, and she struggled to get a grip on it. "You're not dumb," she said fiercely, catching Sheri's hands, forcing the girl to meet her eyes. "You're not useless. Unplanned pregnancies have been happening to women since the beginning of time. You have to tell Jeff."

"I can't. I just . . . can't."

"This is Jeff's baby, too. You have decisions to make. Together." She squeezed Sheri's fingers more tightly. "This problem is not going to go away."

"But—"

"You say you love him, Sheri. Trust is a big part of love. You have to trust him."

"I know." Sheri looked away, battling tears. "But I love him so much. I couldn't bear it if he . . . if he got angry with me. If he . . ." She bit her lower lip.

"What, Sheri? You couldn't bear it if he what?"

"Dumped me."

Sheri had expressed her deepest fear, Alice realized. Of course she expected anger and rejection from Jeff, her parents had never given her anything but.

"Have you ever loved anybody so much?" Sheri asked, slipping her hands from Alice's to brush the tears from her cheeks. "So much you thought you would die if you lost them?"

Hayes. Alice caught her breath as his image flooded her memory, pain with it. Hayes smiling, laughing. Hayes holding her, stroking her, listening to her dreams. Hayes telling her goodbye.

Tears pricked her eyes, and she blinked against them, horrified. How could his rejection still hurt so much now, twelve years after the fact? She shook her head. She'd gotten over her feelings for him long ago.

Sheri shredded the tissue. "Have you, Miss A.?"

"Yes," she answered after another moment, softly. "Once. I was nineteen."

Sheri leaned toward her, distracted for a moment by curiosity. "What happened?"

"He...dumped me. And just like you, I thought I would die when I lost him. I felt like I was dying. But I didn't." She forced a smile. "Obviously."

"But...how did you go on?" Sheri shook her head. "I don't think I could."

Alice thought of those days, their pain, the hopelessness she'd felt. She'd thought they would never end. But they had. Finally.

"I just did," Alice murmured. "And one day I woke up and realized that I was okay. That it didn't hurt so much anymore. After that, with each day I felt better."

"You're stronger than I am, Miss A. I couldn't bear it—I know I couldn't."

Although she believed differently, Alice didn't argue with the girl, but instead shifted the subject again.

"Is Jeff's father part of the reason you're afraid to tell Jeff about the baby?"

Sheri nodded, her eyes flooding with fresh tears. "I told you how he tried to break me and Jeff up. He hates me. He doesn't think I'm good enough for Jeff. When he learns I'm pregnant, I'm afraid he'll find a way to . . . do it. Break us up for good."

Alice drew in a quiet breath, acknowledging the anger she felt every time Sheri talked about Jeff's father. Sheri was a bright and lovely girl. A courageous girl who had overcome great odds to get where she was today. That Jeff's cold, elitist father could reject her simply because of her family situation struck a raw, a personal, nerve in Alice.

Even as she'd worked to help Sheri cope with her hurt over the man's prejudice, she'd wanted to find Mr. High-and-Mighty and give him a piece of her mind.

"Jeff says the other lawyers call him 'Bradford-the-cold-heart.' Jeff can't wait to go off to college to get away from him."

It couldn't be. Alice caught her breath. "Jeff's last name is . . . Bradford?"

"Uh-huh." Sheri drew her eyebrows together, concerned. "Miss A., are you all right?"

"And his father's an attorney?" she asked, ignoring the girl's question, her heart thundering.

Sheri nodded, and Alice sucked in a sharp breath. *Hayes. It couldn't be. But it was.*

The man Sheri had raged about all these months was the same man who had so coldly rejected her. And Sheri's Jeff was little Jeffy. The boy she had once cuddled, the boy she had fantasized would one day call her "Mommy."

She'd often wondered about Jeff, wondered what kind of young man he had grown into, if he had ever thought of her. When she'd known him he had desperately needed a mother and she had desperately needed to be one. She had never forgiven Hayes for allowing her to fall in love with his son. It hadn't been fair to her or to Jeff.

Alice squeezed her fingers into fists. Dear Lord, why hadn't she ever asked Jeff's last name? All these months... she hadn't known.

She lowered her gaze to her clenched hands. Why should she have suspected that Jeff's father was Hayes Bradford, attorney-at-law and coldhearted bastard? After all, it had been twelve years since he'd been a part of her life. And in that time he hadn't sought her out even once.

"Excuse me, Miss A.?"

Alice turned her gaze to the doorway and the young man standing there. "Yes, Rob?"

"Tim's here. Hey, Sheri."

For a moment Alice drew a blank. Then, remembering her next appointment, she forced a smile. "Thanks, Rob. I'll be just a couple more minutes."

"Okay. But—" The boy shifted his gaze to his feet, obviously uncomfortable. "I don't think Tim's... feeling very well today."

Stoned. Again. Alice bit back a sound of frustration and disappointment. They'd all worked so hard to help Tim get straight. "Thanks, Rob. I appreciate the warning."

Sheri grabbed her book bag and jumped up. "If Tim's coming in here high, I'm booking." She shuddered. "He gives me the creeps."

Alice looked at the youngster in surprise. Sheri got along with everybody here at Hope House. She was one of the most well-liked teenagers in the program, and Alice had never heard her speak ill of any of the other kids.

"Is there a problem between you and Tim?"

The teenager shrugged. "I don't know. Not really. It's just that . . ." Sheri caught her bottom lip between her teeth. "There's just something about him that makes me feel kinda . . . funny."

Alice frowned. "Has he ever come on to you or, you know, threatened you in any way?"

Sheri shook her head, then glanced over her shoulder at the door. "No. I gotta go."

Troubled, Alice followed Sheri's gaze. Was this nothing? Or something? She filed that question away for later and forced a smile. "You'll think about what I said? About talking to Jeff?"

The teenager sighed and started for the door. "Yeah. Sure."

"And, Sheri?" The girl stopped and looked back at her. "Don't forget I'm here for you. Okay?"

Sheri hesitated a moment, then nodded and ducked out of the office.

Hayes Bradford stood at Hope House's front gate and gazed up at the rambling, ramshackle old Victorian mansion. So this was where Alice spent her days, he thought. Where the twelve years since he'd seen her last had brought her, where she did her good deeds.

And where they would meet again.

A tightness settled in his chest and Hayes frowned. Twelve years ago he'd made a decision that had been the best for both of them. Especially for her. He made no excuses for that decision; he'd never allowed himself to look back even on the days when he'd missed her so much he had ached.

But he'd hurt her. Badly. And he regretted that with all his heart.

Hayes made a sound of frustration. She'd been too young to see how wrong they'd been for each other, too young to realize the truth about him. About life. They never should have become involved in the first place.

He shook his head. He'd known that at the time, but it hadn't made a bit of difference—he'd been unable to deny his overpowering attraction to her.

It still struck him as crazy. Irrational. He shouldn't have been attracted to her. Everything about her had been foreign to his nature—her background, her age, her outlook on life.

She'd been smart as a whip, with a sharp wit and an even sharper tongue. The chip on her shoulder had rivaled Plymouth Rock in size.

But the wit, tongue and chip, he'd learned, had masked an achingly vulnerable and sensitive young woman. She'd felt everything deeply and to her core. He'd likened her to a prickly pear—prickly on the outside with a sweet, soft center. A center that was easily bruised. Too easily for a man the likes of him.

He drew his eyebrows together, remembering. He'd never understood how she managed it. After the childhood she'd had, after the abuse she'd suffered, how had she managed to remain soft inside? How had she continued to see good in the world and to believe she could better it?

Lord, she'd been beautiful. Fresh and brilliantly alive.

Hayes moved his gaze across the building's front windows. Would she have changed? he wondered. Would he find the same emotional girl he'd known back then? The same girl who had made him remember, if only fleetingly, what it was like to have illusions?

Or would she have grown up? Would life have hardened her clear through—would it have tempered her impossible idealism? He'd wondered about her often over the intervening years; today he would know.

Hayes pushed through the gate and strode up the walk. He shook his head again, this time in an attempt to clear it of the memories tugging at him. Today had nothing to do with his and Alice's past; it wouldn't do for him to forget that. Today he'd come because his son needed him.

Hope House's front door invited him to enter; he did and crossed to the reception desk. The long-haired teenager manning the desk didn't look up. He wore ancient jeans, a threadbare, tie-dye T-shirt and state-of-the-art headphones. Using pencils for drumsticks, the boy pounded out whatever frenetic tune those headphones were blaring just for him.

"Excuse me," Hayes said, moving his hand across the boy's line of vision.

The boy jerked his head up, grinned and popped the headphones off his ears. "Yo, man. What's up?"

What's up? Hayes arched an eyebrow. "I'm looking for the therapist's office."

"That's Miss A. Her office is back there. See?" The boy stood and pointed.

"Is she in?"

"Oh, yeah." The teenager plopped back onto the chair. "She's always in."

Before Hayes could even murmur his thanks, the teenager had returned to his headphones and imaginary drums. Hayes shook his head and started in the direction the would-be musician had indicated. He supposed he should be grateful—his son could look and act like that. His son could be spending his days here instead of with . . . his pregnant girlfriend.

Hayes swore silently. How could Jeff have gotten himself into this situation? Jeff, a National Merit scholar? An all-state athlete? Good God, how could he have been so careless?

Like father like son.

Hayes pulled his mouth into a tight, grim line. How could he judge his son? He'd been much older when the same thing had happened to him. Supposedly wiser. But he and Alice had been lucky. Disaster had been averted by nature.

Lucky. The thought moved through his head, and he twisted his lips. He didn't feel lucky. Not then. Not now. In fact, most times he didn't feel anything at all.

Hayes passed a group of teenagers arguing over a poem, a girl sitting at an easel sketching, past another who appeared to be meditating. When he'd called and questioned Hope House's director about Sheri Kane and her place here, the director had described theirs as a program that used creative self-expression as a vehicle through which troubled teens learned to cope with their problems. Whatever the hell that meant. All he cared about was getting a handle on Sheri Kane so he could take care of Jeff's problem.

He found Alice's office. The door stood ajar. She faced the single window, her back to him. He gazed at her, his mouth suddenly dry, his heart beating fast. Everything about her called to his sensory memory. The curve of her hip, encased now in light-colored denim, reminded him of how his hand had fit over it, as if made just for him. He recalled the feel of her skin, soft, warm, incredibly smooth. The silky sensation of her whiskey-colored hair against his fingers. Lord, how he'd loved to bury his face in it after they'd made love. It had always smelled sweet, like springtime.

Hayes swallowed, fighting against the memories, against the overwhelming sense of déjà vu. He couldn't dispel it, not completely, and frowned. He wouldn't allow himself a trip down memory lane. He wouldn't allow himself, even for a moment, to question the decision he'd made twelve years ago.

As if sensing his presence, Alice turned. Her eyes met his. In that moment he saw that she had changed.

The girl had become a woman.

Hayes skimmed his gaze over her. Some of the changes were subtle, others blatant. Her face bore the signs of maturity, of experience and self-confidence. Her mouth seemed fuller, her figure more lush. The blush of girlhood had been replaced by the bloom of womanhood.

Hayes released a pent-up breath. Twelve years. It had been twelve years since he'd last seen her. Since he'd held her in his arms. Since he'd tasted her mouth, her sultry sweetness.

Twelve years since he'd broken her heart.

She'd never forgiven him. He saw it in her eyes—a trace of vulnerability, of hurt. Of accusation.

Even though he couldn't blame her, he felt bereft, as if he'd lost something really special. Something magical.

He called himself a fool. "Hello, Alice."

She inched her chin up a fraction, and he almost smiled. He remembered that gesture vividly. She'd been forever popping that chin up in defiance or anger. Or when hurt. He wondered which the gesture was in response to now. For she'd changed in another way; now she possessed the ability to hide her real feelings.

"Hello, Hayes."

"Surprised to see me?"

"No." She folded her arms across her chest. "The director mentioned that you called. I figured you'd show up sooner or later."

Hayes stepped into the office, scanning it as he did, taking in the obviously donated furniture, mismatched and worn, the chipped and peeling walls, the desk, haphazardly piled with books, assorted papers and file folders. He brought his gaze back to Alice's. "Then you know why I'm here."

"To inquire about Sheri Kane."

He slipped off his cashmere coat and tossed it over a chair. "I understand you're her therapist."

"We prefer the term 'counselor' here. It makes the kids feel more comfortable."

"Counselor, then." He moved his gaze over the room once more. "I'm not surprised to find you working in a place like this."

She narrowed her eyes. "You say that as if you think being altruistic is a fault. As if wanting to help someone besides myself is something to apologize for."

"Not at all." He arched his eyebrows. "No criticism intended."

"Like hell."

"Picking up right where we left off, I see."

Alice drew in a quick breath, her cheeks burning with color. "We're not picking up anything. You've come about Sheri. Well, I'll tell you what I think. She's a lovely girl, and I'm very fond of her. I don't want to see her hurt any more than she has been already. I consider our relationship privileged, so if you'll excuse me, I have things—"

She started to brush by him; he caught her arm. "She's pregnant. You knew that?"

Alice looked at his hand, then back up at him, eyes narrowed. "Of course. She told me a couple of days ago." Alice shook off his hand. "And Jeff's the father."

"So I understand."

"Life's funny, isn't it, Hayes?"

Hayes's mouth tightened into a hard line, and he swung away from her, crossing to the window. Alice stared at him, at his stiff back, the rigid line of his shoulders, her heart thundering.

Why had she said that? Why had she opened a door best left shut and tightly bolted? Pain trembled through her. And with it regret, so bitter it left her aching and sad.

Hayes Bradford had been a hard man when she'd known him. Unemotional. Coldly determined. Cynical. He'd been the kind of man who walked into a courtroom and owned it, the kind who strode into a room of savvy, successful men and cowed them.

But she'd seen something soft in him. Something emotional. Vulnerable, even. Some part of him that had needed her.

That hint of warmth, of need, had been extinguished in the intervening years, leaving a man dying of the cold. The truth of that pulled at her, even as she told herself that he'd made his own isolation.

He turned back to her, his expression as if chipped from granite. "Is there any chance that Jeff's not the—"

"Father? No chance." Anger moved through her, extinguishing the flutter of sympathy, of empathy. "Sheri is not promiscuous. She and Jeff have been dating for months."

"Exclusively?"

Alice's cheeks burned. "Yes. Exclusively."

"You're angry?"

"Offended."

He lifted his eyebrows. "I don't see anything out of line about my questions. They're questions any parent would ask."

He'd always thought her too open, too emotional. Had always thought her too reactive.

She cocked her chin. "Then why aren't you asking your son these questions? Or weren't his answers the ones you wanted?"

Something flashed in Hayes's eyes, then was gone. "All grown up, I see. Complete with claws."

Anger took her breath. She battled to hold on to it, to keep it from showing. "I was hardly a child back then." But he'd always treated her like one anyway.

"You were nineteen, Alice."

"Of legal age. An adult."

"And I was twenty-seven. Already a widower. Responsible for a young son."

"A son whom I adored. And who adored me."

"We were emotional and philosophical poles apart."

But I loved you anyway. So much I thought I was going to die when you rejected me.

Alice pushed the thought away and inched her chin up a fraction more. "Except in the bedroom. Right? I wasn't too young for you there. I wasn't too philosophically distant then."

"I didn't come here to get into this."

Of course not, she thought. He'd never cared enough about her to come after her. She stiffened her spine. "And what you did come for is inappropriate for me to discuss. Please leave."

He took a step toward her, hand out. "These kids are too young to be thinking about marriage, let alone starting a family."

"By 'these kids' you mean your son?"

Hayes nodded. "He is my main concern. He's the one I care about."

"And I care about Sheri."

"Then help me help them." Hayes made a sound of frustration and turned away from her. For long moments he said nothing, then he turned back to her, his expression strained. "He's infatuated with this girl. He's not thinking clearly."

Blood rushed to Alice's cheeks. And what had been his father's excuse, all those years ago? Had he been infatuated? Had he, too, been confused, his thinking muddled?

"So, you'll think clearly for him," she said, her voice tight with anger.

"It sounds arrogant, but . . . yes. And I'd like your help convincing Sheri to do the right thing."

"What you think is the right thing."

Hayes groaned. "We are the adults."

Alice crossed to the door and swung it wide. "I'm sorry, but you've wasted your time. I believe Sheri and Jeff are old enough to make their own decisions."

"If you were a parent, you'd understand."

Pain at the blow shot through her, and she caught her breath. She had dreamed of being a parent. Once she'd even come close.

Hayes closed the distance between them. Stopping in front of her, he met her eyes. His were dark with regret. "I'm sorry, Alice. I didn't mean to hurt you. Not then. And certainly not now."

She searched his gaze. She didn't want his apologies. Didn't want—or need—his regret. She was doing just fine. And if he hoped for forgiveness, well, some wounds went too deep to heal or forgive.

She narrowed her eyes, pushing aside her hurt, marshaling her anger. "If I were a parent I'd understand? Tell that to the kids I work with here, the kids I try to help deal with the way their older and wiser parents have screwed up their lives and their heads."

His mouth tightened. "That's different. Those aren't the kind of parents I was talking about."

"Oh, I forgot. You're one of those infallible, perfect parents." She drew in an angry breath, then let it out in a rush. "Let's be honest here, Hayes. Your concern has a lot to do with what you think of Sheri. You've tried and sentenced her, yet you know nothing about her. She's intelligent and courageous. And she's been through a hell of a lot. You'd be playing a different tune if Jeff had gotten the daughter of one of your precious senior partners in trouble. Well, I'm not going to help you discriminate against Sheri Kane. Now—'' she indicated the door, her hand shaking so badly she knew he could see ''—please leave.''

He opened his mouth, and she fisted her fingers. ''Now.''

''Fine.'' He plucked his coat from the chair and strode to the door. There he stopped and once again met her eyes. ''Are you so sure it's me who's letting preconceived notions cloud my judgment? Are you sure it's me who's discriminating? Think about it, Alice. I'll be in touch.''

Chapter Two

Alice did think about it. In fact, in the three days since their confrontation, she'd been able to think of little else.

Alice gazed out her office window at the gloomy February day. It seemed impossible to her that spring waited just around the corner. Mardi Gras had come and gone; the first scattered azaleas had burst open, both sure signals of spring. And yet the sky remained flat and gray, the breeze cold and edgy.

Come August, she would long for both, but today a bright-blue sky and mellow breeze would be a comfort.

She touched the cool glass with her fingertips. Had Hayes been right? Was she the one who'd let preconceived notions interfere with judgment? Was she the one who had discriminated?

Alice fisted her fingers on the glass, fighting the wave of denial—and anger—that washed over her. The same wave that had washed over her the other day.

Only the other day she'd been incapable of fighting it.

Where had all that anger come from? She'd looked at Hayes and the emotion had bubbled furiously out of her. If she'd been a fraction less civilized a person, she would have lunged at him.

Frowning, she looked out at Hope House's backyard. Two of her kids had braved the unforgiving breeze and sat huddled together on the bench beneath the huge, old live oak that graced the yard's center. The boy and girl sat facing each other, not speaking, just gazing into the other's eyes, obviously smitten.

How long had it been since she'd felt that way? How long since she'd been willing to brave the cold—or anything else—to be with the man she loved?

Twelve years. Twelve long, empty years.

A lump in her throat, Alice swung away from the view and crossed to her desk. She sank onto the chair and rubbed her temple at the headache that hammered there. She wouldn't think about that now; she couldn't. She had other things she needed to focus on. Like her anger at Hayes.

It hadn't been new emotion; it hadn't been about Sheri and Jeff. Not completely, anyway.

And she hated that. Because she hated what it meant.

She wasn't completely over her feelings for Hayes.

Alice sighed impatiently. Of course she was. She'd recovered from his rejection long ago. She no longer wanted or needed him. She no longer loved him.

She was over everything but her anger.

Obviously. She'd been so busy being angry, she hadn't given him the chance to fully explain why he'd sought her out or to express his thoughts about the pregnancy. She'd tried and convicted him without even allowing him a chance to defend himself.

Just as she'd accused him of doing to Sheri.

She prided herself on being a fair person. On being nonjudgmental. She had to give Hayes that chance. She owed it to Sheri. And Jeff.

Alice grabbed her purse and jumped to her feet. She didn't have an appointment scheduled until one, plenty of time to find Hayes and hear him out. Decision made, she strode to the door.

And collided with Sheri as she raced into the office.

"Sheri!" Alice grabbed the girl's arms to steady her. "I'm so sorry. I didn't see you..."

Alice's words trailed off as she took in the teenager's stricken face. Her heart leaped to her throat. "What's happened?"

Sheri burst into tears. "You've got to help me, Miss A. I don't know what to do. He told. He called my father and...he told him that...I'm..." Sheri dropped her face into her hands. "What am I going to do now?"

Alice slid an arm around the girl's shoulders and led her to the battered couch. Gently she eased her onto it, then pulled a chair over to face her. "Calm down, Sheri. Take a deep breath or two and try to tell me what happened."

The girl nodded, drew in several shaky breaths, then met Alice's eyes.

"He called and told my dad I was pregnant." She curled her fingers into fists in her lap. "I should have known he'd do something like that. I hate him so much. I really do!"

Alice frowned. "Who told?"

"Jeff's dad!"

Hayes had called Sheri's father.

Of course he had. After all, he was the "older and wiser" parent.

She swore silently as guilt shot through her. She, too, should have known Hayes would do something like this. Maybe if she had talked to him, listened to what he'd had to say and had offered advice, this wouldn't have happened. Maybe if she hadn't been so emotional, this could have been avoided.

She laced her fingers in her lap. "How did your dad take it?"

"He took it great," Sheri said sarcastically, her eyes brimming with tears. "Like a real trooper. He called me a...slut and a...a whore. Then he...kicked me out."

The tears spilled over, even though Alice could see how she fought them.

"Did he hit you?" Sheri shifted her gaze away, and Alice touched her hand lightly. "Did he, Sheri?"

The girl met her eyes. Alice's heart twisted at the despair she saw there. And the courage. No seventeen-year-old should know such pain.

"Just once," Sheri whispered. "But I turned real fast so he wouldn't hurt the baby."

Alice caught her breath as anger surged through her, hot and fast, stealing her ability to speak. Body blows to places concealed by clothing was Buddy Kane's *modus operandi.* The bastard.

Sheri clutched Alice's hands. "I don't have anywhere to go...I don't have..." Tears choked her, and she cleared her throat. "What am I going to do, Miss A.? You've got to help me. I don't know what to do."

She burst into tears again, and Alice drew her into her arms. With her Hope House connections, she could find Sheri housing at any number of places in the area. She would be well cared for, off the streets, safe and protected.

But that wasn't good enough.

Professional or not, Sheri needed her. She needed more than a roof over her head and three square meals a day. Sheri needed comfort, understanding, guidance. She needed a friend.

Alice smiled to herself. She would have to clear it with Dennis, the director. And he wasn't going to like it. But she knew him well enough to be certain that, after a moderate argument, he would give his grumbling okay.

And if Sheri's bastard of a father so much as darkened her doorstep, she would slap him with abuse charges so fast he wouldn't know what had hit him.

So much for keeping herself from getting too personally involved.

"You're going to stay with me," Alice said matter-of-factly. "I live alone. I have a guest room."

Sheri tipped her head back, her tear-drenched eyes widening in disbelief. "You'd do that for...me?"

Alice smiled softly. "How can you even ask that? Of course I would."

"But—"

"No buts." Alice plucked her purse from the floor by her chair. "I have to get permission from Dennis. And from your father."

Sheri's eyes widened with fear. "But, Miss A., he—"

Alice patted the girl's hands. "Don't worry, I'll take care of your father. You have your things?"

Sheri nodded, hiccuping, wiping at her wet cheeks. "He chucked them all out in the street. A bunch of the neighbors were out. A few of them . . . laughed."

"Great neighbors," Alice muttered, shaking her head. "You walked here?"

"Hitched."

"We've talked about that, Sheri. It's dangerous. Really dangerous. While you're living with me, you call me for a ride. No hitching. Got it?"

"Sure, but . . . I don't want to cause you any trouble, Miss A. I mean, I don't want to be a pest."

Alice forced an easy smile and hiked her purse onto her shoulder. "You are not going to be any trouble. Come on. I don't have any appointments until one. I'll get you settled in."

And after dealing with Dennis and Buddy Kane, she vowed, she would see Hayes.

Later that afternoon, Alice drew her car to a stop in front of Hayes's large, two-story brick home. The stately house occupied an oversize lot in Mandeville's most exclusive country-club community. She'd always thought it looked like a lawyer's home; it reeked of wealth, social position and the understated elegance born of both.

She'd never been truly comfortable here, maybe because his wife had chosen both the house and its decor, maybe because it was so far removed from her own frame of reference.

Either way, she much preferred her restored Cape Cod-style cottage, her eclectic little street with its hodgepodge of neighbors. Here, everybody was the same as everybody else—well educated, well-bred and well employed, and almost without exception Caucasian, Protestant and Republican. Her neighborhood had variety—a lot of variety—and a lot of life and energy.

Alice swung open the car door and stepped out, a flutter of nervousness in the pit of her stomach. The worst that could happen, she told herself, was that Hayes would tell her to butt out. And she hardly thought he would do that, considering he'd come to her first.

So why was she nervous? She didn't care what he thought of her or her opinions. She had come to help Sheri; she would say her piece and leave.

The front door burst open and a young man slammed through. Jeff, Alice realized, catching her breath, moving her gaze over him. He'd grown into a handsome young man—tall and slim, with the same long face and hawkish features as his father, the same strong chin and light-brown hair streaked with gold. In fact, the resemblance between the father and son was remarkable.

Hayes appeared at the door. "Jeff, come back here immediately. I haven't finished talking to you."

Jeff stopped at the edge of the porch and swung toward his father, his fists clenched. "You weren't talking—you were lecturing! I've had it with your orders. And I've had it with you telling me what to do and how to live."

"I'm your father. I know what's best for you."

"Is that why you called Sheri's father? Was *that* the best thing for me?" Jeff started down the stairs. "Do me a favor, butt out of my life."

"Jeff!" Hayes stepped through the door, and the boy paused. "I forbid you to marry this girl. Do you hear me? I forbid it."

"Forbid?" the boy shouted. "You're not a father. You're a dictator. I'm eighteen, old enough to do what I want. And if I want to marry Sheri, I will." The boy took the last steps in one bound and headed for the garage.

"Jeff!" Hayes stormed across the porch. "Get back here. Now!"

But as Alice could have told Hayes, Jeff neither paused nor acknowledged his father, and a moment later she heard the gun of an engine and the squeal of tires as the teenager backed his car recklessly out of the driveway and into the street. A moment later the teenager roared out of sight.

Alice returned her gaze to Hayes, to his handsome features, etched with a combination of worry and despair. She drew in a deep breath, torn between conflicting emotions. If she approached Hayes now, he would most likely take some of his anger and frustration out on her. He wouldn't be receptive to her suggestions; he would perceive them as criticisms. If she had any sense, she would climb back into her car and drive off.

She'd never been known for leading with her head, and her heart told her that Hayes needed her. He needed an impartial opinion, some sensible advice. His relationship with his son looked to be out of control, and she'd bet her master's degree that he knew it.

Jeff needed her, too. Alice thought of the small, sweet boy she had once cradled in her arms, and her heart twisted. She hated to see him hurting this way. Hated to see him and Hayes at such odds. They needed each other.

Alice started up the flower-lined walk. Foolish or not, appreciated or not, she would offer her opinion and advice. And maybe she would be able to help.

Hayes hadn't moved from his position at the edge of the porch; he still gazed in the direction Jeff had disappeared moments before. As she approached, he turned to her and the unhappiness in his eyes tugged at her heartstrings. She drew in a steadying breath and reminded herself that she'd come to help Sheri and Jeff.

She stopped at the bottom of the steps and tilted her face up to his. "Hello, Hayes."

"Alice," he murmured, his jaw tightening. "I suppose you heard all that?"

She lifted a shoulder. "I didn't mean to eavesdrop."

"But you did anyway." She didn't reply, and he glanced at the street once more. "So now you know the awful truth. My son hates me."

"Actually," she said softly, "I think he loves you very much. That's why he's so angry."

"This isn't a good time, Alice. I'll call you."

Even though he tried, he couldn't quite hide his pain, his frustration. And he hated that, Alice knew. Because he hated weakness, and he perceived emotion as weakness. He always had.

He would like her to leave him alone, give him time to compose himself, to box up and pack away his emotions. To hell with what he would like. She wasn't about to give him the chance to put his armor back into place. She wouldn't be worth her salt as a counselor if she did.

"I remember Jeff as a little boy," she murmured. "He was so sweet. So cuddly. I used to sit for hours and rock him. Do you remember?"

Hayes's mouth tightened and he didn't reply, but Alice could tell by that very stiffening that he did remember. And that it stung. Badly.

She laughed lightly, although the effort hurt. "Truthfully, I liked it as much as he did. Maybe more. I guess we both needed love."

Hayes made a sound of impatience. "Is there some message for me in this little trip down memory lane? Or are you just making small talk?"

Alice looked him in the eye. "He's still that same little boy, Hayes. He needs love. He needs affection."

"Meaning I don't give it to him."

"Meaning you handled that all wrong." The breeze blew her hair across her cheek; she swept it impatiently away. "He's eighteen years old. Too old to drill with orders and expectations. He needs understanding. He needs you to sit down and talk with him, man to man. Like equals. Like friends."

Hayes curved his fingers around the balustrade, so tightly his knuckles whitened. "That's where our thinking differs, Alice. He's not a man. He's still a boy. And I'm not his friend. I'm his father."

She climbed the steps to even their heights. "You're pushing him away when he needs you most."

"You overhear two minutes between us, and suddenly you're an expert on what our relationship is lacking. Oh, that's right," he said sarcastically, "you're a professional."

"Yes, I am." She caught his arm. "If you're going to hang on to your son, you're going to have to learn to give a little. Too much longer, and it'll be too late."

Hayes narrowed his eyes, his look black with fury. "Still trying to create the perfect little family, I see."

She drew in a sharp breath and snatched her hand away. "That was low. But then, you never played fair."

"See, you got out just in time."

She didn't get out of his life. He'd booted her out. Alice worked to hold on to her temper. To the anger that charged through her. "I came to talk about Sheri and Jeff," she said stiffly. "I felt I owed it to them to try to help."

"Help by convincing me to allow Jeff to marry this girl? No way."

"Is that what Jeff wants to do?" she countered. "Does Jeff want to marry Sheri?"

"He doesn't know what he wants to do. He's confused. Truthfully, I don't even know if they've talked about it. He and I have talked about it."

"And you forbade him to marry her."

"Yes." Hayes turned away from her. He crossed to the other side of the porch and stared at the flower garden, brown and barren from the long winter. "Getting married now would ruin Jeff's life. It would ruin both their lives."

"Is that why you called Sheri's father?"

Hayes hesitated, surprised. "How did you—"

"She came to me. Hysterical. He kicked her out."

Hayes uttered an oath and looked away. "I felt her parents should know. I thought we could talk, come up with a mutually agreeable solu—"

"Mutually agreeable solution!" Furious, Alice crossed the porch to face him. "Did you plan to meet Buddy Kane at the club for a drink? Like two civilized adults? You don't know anything about Sheri or her situation! You know nothing about her father. Buddy Kane doesn't bluff. He doesn't think before he reacts, and he reacts like an animal."

"I didn't mean to cause her trouble," Hayes said quietly, looking shaken. "And I had no idea she hadn't told her parents."

"That's right, you had no idea. Why do you suppose she's part of the Hope House program? What did you think her problems were? And what did you think was their source?"

"Wait a minute. You stand here accusing me. What about you?" He took a step toward her, stopping so close she had to tilt her head back to meet his eyes. "If you had talked to me the other day, this wouldn't have happened. I would have asked your opinion—I would have known what Sheri's home situation was. But you were too busy being angry at me about our past to hear me out."

She wanted to deny his words, but couldn't. She stuffed her trembling hands into her blazer pockets, fighting off the guilt rushing through her. "Shifting the blame, Counselor? But that's a lawyer's stock-in-trade, isn't it?"

"I think you're too blinded by your personal feelings to see what's best in this situation."

"That's ridiculous!" She inched her chin up. "As you pointed out a minute ago, I'm a professional. I don't let my personal feelings interfere with my judgment."

"I agreed to marry you, Alice. Even though I didn't think it was the right thing for any of us."

Alice took an involuntary step back from him, stunned. He'd laid it right between them, out in the open. He'd always been brutally direct. Coldly honest.

She sucked in a quick breath, battling tears, battling the urge to fling herself against him and pummel him with her fists. "You were honorable. You did your duty. But when I lost our baby, you rescinded your offer."

"I never meant to hurt you." He reached a hand out to her, then dropped it. "Your hurt would have been much greater had we stayed together. Surely you see that now."

"Now that I'm older and wiser?" To her horror tears flooded her eyes, threatening to fall. She fought them back. "Was your decision best for Jeff, too? He was happy, Hayes."

For one long moment, Hayes said nothing. Then he shook his head. "He'd grown so close to you, so fast. I couldn't believe how quickly he bonded with you."

"Is that why you ended our relationship? Because Jeff was growing to love me? Because he needed me?"

Hayes's expression twisted with pain. "You must think me as much of a bastard as Jeff does." He turned away from her and gazed out at the elegantly landscaped yard. "I hated doing that to him. The way he missed you broke my heart."

But that was the only thing that had broken Hayes's heart. Losing her certainly hadn't.

"He's never forgiven me, I don't think." Hayes turned his gaze to hers. "And neither have you."

Alice stared at him, her mouth dry, her heart fast. "No," she whispered. "I guess I haven't."

Without another word, she turned and walked away.

Hayes watched Alice go, his chest heavy and aching. He wanted to call her back, wanted to so badly her name formed on the tip of his tongue, begging to jump off. He opened his mouth, then closed it. What more did they have to say to each other? He'd already hurt her too much.

He curved his fingers into fists, remembering her expression of moments ago. The way her eyes had welled with tears, the way her mouth had trembled. Remembering her question, *Is that why you ended our relationship? Because Jeff loved me? Because he needed me?*

She did think him a coldhearted bastard. Just as Jeff did.

But isn't that what he'd wanted? To push her away? To keep her and the whole damn world at arm's length?

But she'd gotten close anyway. Even after he'd struck out at her with every weapon in his verbal arsenal. She'd always had that ability. Had always been able to stand up to him.

He admired that in her, admired her pluck.

Hayes swore. If only his feelings stopped with admiration. They didn't. She'd always been able to stir his emotions. And senses. He breathed deeply through his nose. The scent of her perfume, something at once quixotic and mysterious, lingered, and his senses swam with it.

Whatever irrational chemistry had existed between them twelve years ago existed between them still. At least for him. As she'd faced him only moments before, he'd wanted to hold her, to touch her—even though they'd both been blazingly angry, even though he knew they were wrong for each other.

She'd been gone minutes already, yet the want pulled at him still. He swore again. Twelve years ago he'd given in to the pull, and in the process had almost ruined all their lives.

Jeff.

Hayes turned and strode into the house, not stopping until he reached the back deck. He frowned. He was losing Jeff. He saw it, he felt it, and yet he had no idea how to stop the deterioration of their relationship. He'd worked on them being together, scheduling plenty of father-and-son time, thinking that if they spent more time together they would grow closer. Instead the opposite had happened.

The deck overlooked the golf course's third hole, and as he watched, a golfer approached the tee and prepared to swing. The man wheeled back and hit the ball, with obvious force but no finesse. The ball sliced badly to the right and into the rough. The golfer teed up and did the same thing again, probably believing that if he flailed at the ball enough times it would finally bend to his will.

But it never would, Hayes thought. That golfer could flail at the ball a thousand times, and never get it right.

Would he ever get it right with Jeff? Or would he spend the rest of his life doing it all wrong, missing the mark every time?

Swearing, Hayes stooped and picked up a pine cone from the deck and flung it toward the golf course. He could walk into a courtroom, present a series of arguments and sway a jury or convince a judge. It was easy; he rarely lost.

But in personal relationships, he always lost. He always *felt* lost.

Thoughts of his wife, of his disastrous marriage, flooded his mind before he could stop them, before he could prepare himself. When he'd met her she'd been an outgoing and ambitious law student. They'd had similar backgrounds, similar goals. She'd seemed the perfect choice of life mate.

But their union had been a disaster. She'd been too emotional, he too cold. She'd needed something from him he hadn't known how to give her; for her, their relationship had always lacked something essential. Her occasional moodiness had become bouts of black depression after they'd married, intensifying with Jeff's birth.

He'd worked hard to try to make her happy. To try to make the marriage work. Not hard enough. Obviously. One day he'd gotten a call at the office. Isabel had run her car off the side of a bridge. It had been ruled an accident, even though the coroner had determined that she'd ingested a huge amount and variety of pills, probably just before getting behind the wheel.

Hayes flexed his fingers, remembering how stunned, how shocked he'd been. How hurt. He frowned. But it had been Jeff who had really been hurt. Jeff who had suffered. He'd vowed never to put Jeff in that kind of emotional danger again.

Yet he had—almost. With Alice.

And even though he'd saved them all just in time, Jeff had seen it as another betrayal. Another rejection. Another way his father had let him down.

Too much longer, Hayes, and it will be too late. You'll have lost him for good.

The truth of Alice's words burned in his gut. What would he do if he lost him? Hayes wondered, staring blindly out at the golf course. What would he do if it was already too late?

Unable to face the answers, Hayes turned and went inside.

Chapter Three

Sheri awakened with a start. She pulled herself into a sitting position and, disoriented, glanced around the cheery, old-fashioned bedroom. Miss A.'s guest room, she thought. That's right. She saw her math book upside down on the floor by the bed and remembered: she'd been studying for her geometry quiz. She must have fallen asleep.

Sheri reached for the textbook. She'd been so tired lately. Bone tired. Staying awake during class, especially math and science, had been nearly impossible. But the doctor had said that would pass. As would her queasy stomach.

Yawning, Sheri leaned back against the mountain of feather pillows propped up behind her, snuggling into them. She really liked it here at Miss A.'s. Everything was so clean and sweet smelling. Nothing fancy or expensive looking, just...nice. Comfortable. Like Miss A.

Sheri smiled and smoothed her fingers over the delicately colored old quilt. A wedding-ring design, Miss A. had called it. Made by hand a hundred years ago. Sheri tilted her head. Silly, she knew, but the quilt made her feel...hopeful. Like everything was going to turn out okay.

A scuffling sound came from the window, and she jerked her gaze to the dark rectangle of glass. Just as she thought she'd imagined the sound, a face appeared at the window. A scream flew to her lips, her hand to her chest.

Then she realized who it was.

Jeff.

She scrambled off the bed and raced across the room. She unlatched the window and, as quietly as she could, slid it up. "You scared me to death," she whispered, unhooking the screen. "What are you doing here?"

"Trying my best not to break my neck."

She peeked past the window ledge. Jeff stood on a clay pot propped on top of a rickety old lawn chair. Every few seconds he had to sort of rotate his hips to keep from falling. She giggled. "I see that. But why are you here?"

"Can I come in?"

Her smile faded, and she searched his troubled expression. "What's wrong?"

"I had to see you." He caught her hands and brought them to his mouth, almost losing his balance as he did. "I had to be with you. Please, let me come in."

Sheri glanced over her shoulder. Light glowed from the crack beneath the door, and she heard faint strains of music from the other room. She bit her lip, torn. "I don't know... Miss A.'s still up."

"I'll be a perfect gentleman. And quiet as a mouse." He grinned, and the dimples she found irresistible cut his cheeks. "Scout's honor."

She couldn't resist him, and he knew it. She saw it in his eyes. With a shake of her head, she held up the screen so Jeff could pull himself in. Once inside, he caught her to him, curving his arms tightly around her.

"God, Sheri, I love you so much."

She slipped her arms around him. The cold air clung to his sweater and jeans, chilling her through her thin gown. "I love you, too, Jeff. So much it scares me."

Easing away from her, he cupped her face in his palms. "Don't be scared, babe. We're going to be okay. I know it."

"Oh, Jeff..." She lifted her face in invitation, and he caught her mouth. They kissed, one long, drugging exchange after another.

He dragged his mouth to her ear. "I want you so bad," he murmured. "It hurts."

"I know..." She arched as he moved his hands down her back until he cupped her bottom. "I want you, too."

He groaned. "But we shouldn't. Not now. Not here."

"No," she repeated, curling her fingers around his shoulders, denial almost painful. She longed to lie with him and cling to him, longed for the safe feeling being with him gave her. Being with him would assure her, even if only for those minutes, that everything was going to be all right. "We can't."

"I don't know what I'd do if I lost you, Sheri."

"I'd die without you. I know I would."

He groaned again and rested his forehead against hers. "I had a fight with my old man this afternoon. I haven't been back."

A shudder of apprehension moved through her, and she tightened her fingers. "The fight was about me, wasn't it? And about the baby?"

He shifted his gaze. "Partly."

"Tell me the truth, Jeff."

"Come on." He laced their fingers and led her to the bed. They climbed onto it and cuddled together against the pillows. After a moment, Jeff made a sound of frustration. "He forbade me to...see you."

She caught her breath. "Oh, Jeff."

He curved his arm tighter around her. "Don't worry," he said grimly. "He can't keep me away from you. No matter what he does."

Sobs welled in her chest and throat. "Why does he...hate me so much? What have I done to him?"

Jeff pulled her closer. "It's not you, babe. It's me. He thinks I'm a baby. He treats me like one. Like I can't think for myself, like I always make the wrong decisions."

Jeff rubbed his cheek against her hair, and she sighed in contentment.

"He has my future all mapped out. He has my career planned. My life. What about what I want?" He met her eyes, the expression in his anguished. "What about what I feel?"

She reached up and stroked his cheek, liking the tickle of the beginnings of his beard. "At least he cares," she whispered. "At least he loves you."

"Does he?" Jeff shook his head. "I'm not so sure."

"He wants the best for you." She cleared her throat. "He's certain I'm not it. That our baby isn't it."

"Then he's wrong. I know you're the best thing for me. I know it." He cupped her face in his palms again. "I'm of legal age now. He can't tell me what to do anymore."

"What about school?" She took a deep breath. "What about Georgetown? Your plans are set. And without your dad's support..." She let the words trail off, apprehension and misery settling in the pit of her stomach. "What are we going to do, Jeff? What are we going to do about...you know, the baby?"

He dropped his hands and looked away. "I don't know yet."

"I see," she said, her voice pinched.

"Don't sound like that. There's nothing to see. I just don't know yet."

Sheri laid a hand protectively over her abdomen. "I won't have...an abortion. We haven't talked about this, but I won't. I love this baby...I want it. I couldn't—"

"I know." He covered her hand. "And I wouldn't ask you to, Sheri. Not ever."

"Then what are we going to do?" She met his eyes, tears trembling in hers.

He shook his head. "I have to think about this. I have to make a plan."

"Jeff, I'm scared. I have this terrible feeling." The tears spilled over. "I'm afraid that something's going to happen to us. That something's—"

"Shh..." He smoothed the tears off her cheeks. "Let's not talk about this now. I need a little time, that's all. Everything's going to be okay. I promise."

She nodded, even as a sob shuddered past her lips.

He caught her to him. "I love you, Sheri. I do. You've got to believe me. I'm not going to let anything bad happen—"

A knock sounded on the bedroom door, and Alice poked her head in. "Sheri, are you all…righ…" Alice stared at Jeff, stunned silent.

The teenagers sprang guiltily apart. "We weren't doing anything, Miss A.!" Sheri said, her voice shaking and her cheeks hot with color. "Just talking."

"Don't blame her," Jeff chimed in, obviously as uncomfortable as Sheri. "It's my fault. I begged her to let me come in."

"I hope you're not mad." Sheri wrung her hands. "I didn't… I only…"

Sheri's voice faded. She looked at Jeff, but he stared at Alice, a puzzled expression on his face.

Alice returned his steady gaze, her chest tight. Little Jeffy. She couldn't believe how much he resembled Hayes. She couldn't believe that, after all these years, he sat in her guest room, all grown up.

Alice cleared her throat. "Do you remember me, Jeff?"

He cocked his head, frowning. "You do look kind of familiar."

Sheri glanced from Jeff to Alice and back, obviously confused. "You two know each other?"

Alice met Sheri's gaze. "I dated his father a long time ago. Jeff was only five."

"Holy… cow. It is you."

"Why didn't you tell me?" Sheri's expression shifted from confused to accusing. "You should have told me."

"I only realized the other day when you mentioned Jeff's last name and the fact that his father's a lawyer."

"But that was *days* ago."

"And a lot's happened in those few days." Alice looked at Jeff once more and smiled softly. "After I ... went away, I really missed you. I hope you knew that."

"Yeah, I knew." Jeff's expression stiffened. "Breaking up was my dad's doing. Not yours. He told me."

Alice had to admire Hayes's honesty. It would have been so much easier, she knew, for Hayes to tell his young son that *she* had done the dumping. But then, Hayes had always been brutally honest.

"He let me keep a picture, though."

Alice's throat closed with emotion. "A picture?"

"Of you and me. That time at the zoo. We rode the camel together." He shrugged, all adult nonchalance. "You probably don't remember."

"Oh, my," she whispered, knowing how inane that sounded, but too moved to say any more. She blinked against the prick of tears at the back of her eyes. She did remember that day. Clearly. It had been just after she'd learned she was pregnant, just after Hayes had proposed. It had been when she still believed she and Hayes would have a happy ending.

Jeff was eyeing her expectantly, and she forced a shaky smile. "On the contrary, Jeff, I remember that day very well."

"I still have the picture ... somewhere. Maybe I'll ... bring it by sometime?"

"I'd like that," she said softly. "I'd like it a lot."

A momentary silence fell between them. Sheri filled it. "I can't believe you didn't tell me," she said again, frowning. "We've seen each other since then. A bunch of times."

She didn't have an excuse for not telling Sheri, Alice realized. Not a good one. Sheri didn't trust easily, the bond they'd formed was extremely fragile. And keeping this information from her—even though harmlessly intended—had shaken that trust.

Guilt plucked at her. She hadn't wanted to share her feelings. She hadn't wanted the girl to know how much she had loved Hayes or how badly he'd hurt her. And she wouldn't have been able to hide it.

She hadn't been fair. She asked Sheri to share everything with her. She insisted to the girl that they had a mutually trusting relationship. She realized that wasn't completely true. And the hell of it was, Sheri probably realized it, too.

"Would you mind if we talked about it later?"

Sheri shrugged and looked away. "I guess."

"Thanks. And, Sheri?" The girl met her eyes once more. "I'm not your father and you don't have to sneak around with me. Our guests call at the front door."

The girl colored. "Yes, ma'am."

"And speaking of fathers..." Alice turned to Jeff. "Does yours know where you are?" When Jeff shook his head, she arched her eyebrows in question. "Are you going to call him or should I? He has a right to know where you are. I'm sure he's worried sick."

His expression tight, Jeff climbed off the bed. "He's my father—I'll call."

"You can use the phone in the kitchen. Sheri—" she turned to her young charge "—slip into a robe and come on out. I'll retire so you and Jeff can visit in the living room."

In the end, they all sat in the living room, talking and listening to the Cajun music that Alice loved. Jeff's call to Hayes was short and, from what Alice inadvertently overheard, terse. When he reappeared in the living room, his tight expression testified to the fact that the call had not gone well.

Sheri looked at Jeff nervously. "Everything okay?" she asked, making room for him beside her on the couch.

"Yeah," he answered, shrugging with what seemed to Alice to be forced negligence. "No sweat."

An hour later, Alice discovered her instincts had been correct. The call had not gone well, and everything was certainly not okay. Hayes stood on her front porch, looking ready to explode.

After darting a quick glance toward the living room and the teenagers, Alice slipped outside, softly shutting the door behind her. She leaned against it and tipped her head back to meet his eyes. "Don't do this, Hayes."

"Don't do what?" he snapped. "I've come for my son. That's all."

"I know." She felt his anger and frustration as an almost palpable thing. It crackled in the air around them. She touched his sleeve lightly, attempting to reassure, to calm. "You're upset. So is he. If you go in there now, you're both going to say things you'll regret."

"I didn't know where the hell he was. All day, Alice. And after the way he left, the mood he was in...I was afraid ...I thought maybe he'd been..." He choked the words, the thought, back, his mouth tightening. "Dammit to hell. Anything could have happened."

"I know how you must have felt. How you must feel still." She moved her fingers rhythmically across his arm, stroking, soothing. He hadn't taken the time to put on a coat, and his cashmere sweater was soft under her fingers, his flesh beneath the fabric hard and warm. Realizing what she was doing, she dropped her hand. "Let him be anyway, Hayes. Let him have this moment of independence."

Hayes hesitated, obviously torn. "This is crazy. It's out of control. And even though I can see that, I haven't a clue how to fix it."

Alice's heart went out to him. He was a man who avoided emotion, a man accustomed to being able to "fix" whatever he set his mind to. And now he found himself mired in an emotionally explosive situation that no amount of coolheaded reasoning could fix.

"Jeff's going through a crisis right now," she said softly. "He's growing up. Facing the prospect of graduation, of going to college in the fall. He's becoming independent. Or trying to. That's hard." She caught herself reaching out to touch him again and twined her fingers together. "To top it off, now he has to adjust to the idea of becoming a father himself. Give him this moment. He's here. He's safe."

For long seconds, Hayes gazed at her, considering, weighing his options. He nodded. "Okay. I'll leave him in your care. But I want him home by midnight."

She smiled, relief spiraling through her. "Fair enough. I'll talk to him and—"

The door swung open, flooding the porch with light, illuminating Hayes's tense face. Alice turned, even though she knew without a doubt who stood behind her. She took one look at Jeff's expression, and her stomach sank. This was not going to be pretty.

"Before either of you say anything," she said quickly, "try to—"

"I should have known," Jeff interrupted, furious. "I should have known you wouldn't take me at my word. I said I'd be home directly, but you had to come chasing after me."

"That was over an hour ago, son. Exactly how do you define 'directly'?"

"You tell me. You try to tell me everything else I should do and feel."

Hayes made a sound of disgust. "Give me a break. You want to be treated like a man? Act like one. A man is only as good as his—"

"Word," Jeff filled in, mimicking his father. "A man takes responsibility for his actions. A man is strong and never gives up or makes excuses. I've heard all this a million times."

"Really?" Hayes took a step toward his son, eyes narrowed. "Could have fooled me, young man."

"Go to hell."

Jeff wheeled around and strode inside. Hayes stormed after him, catching the door with the palm of his hand, aware of Alice following close behind.

He reached the living room and stopped in surprise. Sheri sat on the couch, a throw pillow clutched to her stomach. He glanced back at Alice questioningly.

She lifted her shoulders. "She's staying with me."

"Hello, Mr. Bradford," the girl squeaked, obviously terrified.

Hayes struggled to hold his anger at Jeff in check. He forced a stiff smile. "Hello, Sheri. You're looking well."

"You mean she's looking pregnant," Jeff spat, clenching his fists.

Hayes swung his gaze toward his son, his eyebrows lowered ominously. "I did not mean that. I meant she's looking well."

"Don't, Jeff," Sheri pleaded. "Leave it alone."

"Stay out of this, Sheri. It's between me and my dad." He laid a hand on her shoulder as if to relieve the sting of his words. "You didn't know she was staying here, did you? Where did you think she was going to go after she got kicked out? Because of you. Because you couldn't leave well enough alone."

Hayes grimaced. "I didn't mean to mess things up for you, Sheri. That wasn't my intention at all. I'm sorry."

The girl's eyes filled with tears, and Hayes's chest tightened. For nothing more than an apology, she actually appeared grateful. Like a stray puppy exuberant over the tiniest bit of kindness or attention, even when offhand.

"That's okay, Mr. Bradford," she whispered. "It wasn't your fault."

"It was his fault, Sheri," Jeff countered, furious. "He can't stand that you and I have each other. He'd like nothing better than to drive a wedge between us. Isn't that right, Attorney Bradford?"

"I've had enough of this," Hayes said, making a slicing motion with his right hand. "You're my son. You live under my roof. I expect you home in thirty minutes." He nodded at Sheri and Alice, then started for the door.

"Hey, Dad," Jeff called. Hayes stopped at the door and looked over his shoulder at his son. "When I telephoned, didn't you question why I was here? Did you think I'd just come to visit your old girlfriend, the one you dumped because you thought she was too much like Mom?"

Hayes sucked in a quick, sharp breath, his son's words ricocheting through him, making him feel as if he'd just been punched squarely in the gut. He shot a glance at Alice; she, too, looked as if she'd been slapped.

He swore silently, battling for control. He didn't want Alice hurt again. He didn't want her dragged into his and Jeff's problems. Unfortunately, Jeff didn't have the same compunctions.

Grasping the doorknob, he said, "Thirty minutes, son. No more."

Hayes let himself out. As he snapped the door shut behind him, he drew in a deep, painful breath. His son's words had hurt. Just as Jeff had intended when he'd hurled them at him. His son had known just where to strike to inflict the deepest, bloodiest wound.

Had Jeff learned that from him? Hayes wondered. Had his son watched him, listened and absorbed, just as he had with his own father? And would he end up in the same place at thirty-nine years old, alone save for an all-consuming career and a son who despised him?

Emotion choking him, Hayes crossed the narrow gallery to its edge. Alice's street, with it row of mostly restored cottages, faced the Tchefuncte river. The sleepy river wound its way through the community of Madisonville and beyond, lovely and wild. Hayes stared out at the quiet water, grateful for the dark, for the way the night enveloped him.

He wasn't losing Jeff.

He'd lost him already.

Hayes curved his hands around the gallery railing, fighting the emotion that raged inside him, just as he'd fought it all his life. Only this time he couldn't control it. It barreled through him, leaving him feeling impotent, powerless to battle this thing happening between him and his son.

Hayes heard the creak of the door a moment before the sliver of light fell across the porch, penetrating the darkness. *Alice.* He closed his eyes, drinking in the scent of her perfume, the cadence of her quiet breathing and the way both moved over him like warm water.

"Hayes?"

He turned and met her gaze. She stood with the light behind her, her face in shadow. He sensed rather than saw the empathy in her eyes.

She shut the door quietly and crossed the gallery. When she reached him, she caught his hand and laced their fingers. "Come."

She led him across the street, to the dark riverbank. For long moments they stood side by side, not speaking, listening to the gentle lap of the water against the shore.

Alice tipped her face up to his. "I'm sorry. I know how much that must have hurt."

He touched his fingers to her cheek. Her skin was soft and warm. Real. He moved his hands to her hair, rubbing the silky strands between his fingers, remembering.

They had shared only a matter of months of their past and yet in this moment he felt bound to her. Connected, as if Jeff had been theirs and they had shared all their lives. As if they had no secrets from each other.

And it felt good. Damn good.

He didn't question the feeling, but instead let it flow dangerously, languorously, over him. He brought his other hand to her cheek and cupped her face. "You're so beautiful. I always thought you the most radiant woman I'd ever known."

"Hayes?" she whispered, her voice thick. "What—"

He bent his head and brushed his mouth against hers. Lightly. With a tenderness he'd thought himself no longer capable of. She trembled beneath his hands, and he drew a ragged breath, longing to hold her against him, to kiss her hotly and deeply, to possess her mouth and then, once again and at long last, her body.

Instead he dropped his hands and moved away from her. "What's happened to me and Jeff?" he asked softly, gazing out at the dark water. "What's happened to the boy who looked up to me?" He glanced over his shoulder at her. "Do you remember, Alice? He used to seek my approval. He used to think I was...special. Larger than life."

"I remember," she murmured.

Hayes's voice thickened, and he shook his head. "He used to call me 'Daddy.' Now he doesn't call me...anything. Why is he so angry with me?"

She didn't have an answer, he knew. Only he and Jeff did.

With a sound of frustration, he crossed to the very edge of the riverbank. Stooping, he scooped up a rock, then flung it as hard as he could out at the water. It hit and broke the surface, violating the quiet.

"This isn't what I wanted for him, you know." Hayes looked briefly toward the star-strewn sky, then met her gaze once more. "I wanted everything wonderful for him, and I wanted it to be easy. I wanted it to be perfect."

She closed the distance between them. "But it's life, Hayes. And it's never perfect. All you can do is be the best parent you know how to be."

"And when that's not good enough?"

She gazed at him for a long moment, then lifted her shoulders. "Then it's not."

He laughed, the sound tight with derision. "That's just great. Because no matter how we try, some of us just aren't good enough."

"You're being too hard on yourself."

"Am I?"

"Yes." She took another step closer. "We both know the world is full of parents who don't even care enough to try. And there are parents who are more despicable even than that."

"And that doesn't have a thing to do with the kind of parent I am or the ways I screwed up." He met her gaze evenly, though it hurt. He would hate it if he saw pity in her eyes or, worse, condemnation. "Isabel never rocked Jeff. She was too caught up in her own unhappiness. Her own pain. After you . . . were gone, I rocked him. Or tried to. But he didn't want me—he didn't like it when I held him that way."

Swearing, Hayes swung away from her. "You can't imagine how much that hurt. You can't imagine how—" Hayes bit back the words. "I tried to make up for Isabel's leaving him. For her not loving him. I tried the only way I knew how. But it wasn't good enough. Not by a long shot."

"But you tried."

"And failed. Just like I did with Isabel." He clenched his hands. "She was so unhappy. I should have forced her to get counseling. After the first few times dragging her there, I gave up. And then... and then she was dead."

"And you believe she took her own life? Even though the coroner ruled it an accidental death? Even though her insurance company paid up?"

"I can't be certain," Hayes said, rubbing his temple wearily. "But you tell me why else an intelligent, educated woman takes a medicine cabinetful of pills and a stiff drink, then gets into a car. I'll never forgive Isabel for leaving us that way. For leaving Jeff with that terrible legacy."

Silence stretched between them for long moments. Alice broke it first. "What he said in there—was it true?" Hayes met her eyes, then looked away. She caught his arm, forcing him to face her again. "Did you end our relationship because you thought I was like Isabel?"

Hayes paused, then shook his head. "Jeff was five. He's gotten confused over the years. He—"

"He had to have gotten the idea somewhere. Is it true?" she asked again. "Did you end it because you thought I was like Isabel?"

For long moments he said nothing, then he murmured. "You know why I ended it. I didn't lie to you, Alice."

"You thought I was too young."

"You *were* too young." He cupped her face in his palms. "You had your whole life ahead of you. You didn't need to be saddled with me or Jeff. With our problems."

"Saddled," she repeated, stunned, hurt. "If you actually think that, then you know nothing about passion. About love or the need to connect with other people. I loved you. I loved Jeff. I wanted the responsibility. With all my heart."

"That was youth talking then. Rose-colored memories now. You wanted to create the perfect little family. But you'd never have had it with me. Because I would never have given you what you needed to survive. To be happy. I'm incapable of it, Alice."

"Rose-colored memories?" She jerked free of his grasp. "This is such a bunch of bull. Tell me the truth, Hayes. You thought I would never have given *you* what you needed. Isn't that right? Isn't that what you think still?"

"You're wrong. Dead wrong." He took a step toward her, hand out. "If I could just make you see that, you wouldn't be angry anymore. If I could make you—"

"Just like you want to make Jeff see what's right? Make him believe what you know is correct?" She took a step back, shaking her head. "You've been delivering closing arguments so long, Counselor, you're actually starting to believe them. Well, deliver them to someone else, because I'm not buying."

She started back to her cottage. Hayes watched her go, his chest tight, a dozen different denials on the tip of his tongue. Did she really believe he'd ended their relationship because she lacked? Because he'd wanted something better?

Didn't she know he'd never had anything better? That going on without her had been hell?

She reached her porch with its welcoming windows, then her front door. Hand on the knob, she stopped and looked back at him.

He couldn't see her face, her expression. But something passed between them, strong and sad. He opened his mouth to call out to her, but his throat closed over the words. A moment later she was gone.

Turning his back to her lighted windows, he walked to his car.

Chapter Four

Six days later Alice stood in front of her bathroom mirror, putting the finishing touches on her hair and face. She frowned into the mirror. The days since her encounter on the riverbank with Hayes had been hell. She hadn't been able to put him out of her mind, hadn't been able to forget the few stunning moments when his lips had been upon hers. Those moments had interfered with her work and invaded her sleep. She'd awakened every morning feeling unrested and achy.

She wanted him to kiss her again.

A kiss? Her frown deepened. Could she even call the way he'd brushed his mouth against hers a kiss? His touch had been as light as the whisper of butterfly wings against her flesh. Hardly the fevered meeting found in movies and romance novels.

She picked up her brush and ran it through her hair. And she'd felt faint with pleasure. His kiss had swamped her senses, stolen her ability to speak, to protest. It had stolen her free will.

That lightest of kisses had stolen her last six days.

Alice paused, the brush in midstroke. After twelve years, after he'd broken her heart, Hayes could still move her with no more than the faintest of touches.

Why? Why this man and no other? Did she possess some flaw in her character that made her want to be hurt again? Because Hayes would hurt her. He'd never loved her. He never would.

Love? She dropped her hand, and the brush slipped from her fingers, clattering onto the tile counter. She didn't love Hayes; she didn't yearn for him to love her. She'd recovered from such silliness long ago.

But she had loved him once, deeply and with all her heart. And he'd rejected her.

And that's what it came down to, plain and simple. It didn't matter if all those years ago he'd thought her too young, or too much like Isabel, or even that she wasn't good enough for him. The truth was, he hadn't loved her. If he had, he wouldn't have let her go.

Why had he kissed her? Why, after all the time that had passed, had he chosen to turn her world upside down with a kiss?

The sex between them had always been good. Great, even. In the bedroom they had never had conflicts; it had been as if they were made for each other.

As she gazed at herself, color climbed her cheeks, wanton and feminine. She swore silently. That wasn't enough for her anymore, she told herself determinedly. No matter how Hayes stirred her physically, she would not open herself for another rejection.

Turning her back on her reflection and telltale blush, she went to the living room to collect her purse and keys. This morning the entire Hope House faculty was meeting to discuss Tim Benson's continued drug problem. Dennis had called the meeting, and she suspected he was going to advise that Tim be dropped from the program. Hope House had a strict no-drugs policy, and Tim had broken it time and again.

Yet she was undecided about how she was going to vote. Which presented a problem. As the counselor on staff, several of the faculty would look to her for a lead.

She plucked her purse from beside the coffee table and rummaged through it for her keys. She was torn between wanting to help the boy and admitting he needed a different, more rigorous kind of program.

She paused in her search. Sheri's uneasiness about Tim had continued to bother her. Did some of the other kids feel the same way Sheri did? Had they picked up on something she'd missed in her weekly sessions with Tim? Something dangerous?

For the program to work, the kids had to feel safe at Hope House. The faculty had worked to create a comfortable, nurturing environment. For some of these kids, like Sheri, it was the first time they'd experienced that kind of environment. If one student made the others feel uncomfortable or threatened, the program would fail.

She found the keys and started for the door. She worried what would happen to Tim if they let him go. To Tim it wouldn't matter that he'd repeatedly broken the rules or that he was unhappy in the program; he would see it as a rejection. And so many people in his life had already rejected him, including his family. Tim Benson was a deeply troubled young man.

The phone rang, and Alice glanced quickly at her watch. Although behind schedule, she went back to catch it, thinking it might be Dennis or another of her Hope House colleagues. "Hello," she answered, glancing at her watch again.

Nothing. Just dead air.

"Hello," she repeated. Again no one responded, although she heard breathing on the other end. Chill bumps raced up her arms, and she dropped the phone back into its cradle. Someone had been on the other end of the line, hanging there, listening, waiting.

It wasn't the first such call she'd had in the past couple of weeks.

Silly, Alice told herself, rubbing her arms. She was being silly. The caller had dialed a wrong number and hadn't been polite enough to say so. It happened all the time.

Sure. Rubbing her arms again, she slipped into her jacket and started for the door. As she reached it, the phone rang again. Even though she told herself she was overreacting, she didn't make a move toward it. It rang a second time, then a third. Her machine picked it up on the fourth ring.

And her foster mother's cheery voice floated through the house. *"Hey, Alice. Where've you been? Give me a call."*

As the machine clicked off, Alice made a sound of self-directed amusement. So much for mysterious callers. She let herself out of the house. She would return Maggie's call after the meeting. And they would have a laugh at Alice having been afraid to answer the phone.

* * *

Hayes swung his car door open and stepped out into A Coffee and Pastry Place's parking lot. The coffeehouse's windows glowed warmly in the fading light, beckoning him.

As Alice beckoned him. Now. As she had all week.

Swearing softly, he slammed the car door. He couldn't stop thinking about her. Over the past seven days, the things they'd said to each other had replayed in his mind over and over. And with them, the way she'd looked at him the moment before she'd walked away. Bruised and angry.

He'd wanted to call her back, had longed to drag her into his arms, to capture her mouth with his.

Hayes tipped his head back, his face to the purpling sky. He never should have kissed her. Never should have given in to the temptation of her sweet mouth.

That one brief touch had sent his sensory memories spinning into sharp focus, his control slightly out of reach. Lord, but he'd loved touching her. Holding her. Making love with her.

He flexed his fingers. Dammit. He wished it were as simple as sex. He was no roving adolescent; he could keep a lid on his libido. The truth was, he wasn't sure why he was here, why he'd been unable to stop himself from seeking her out.

He'd told himself he wanted to talk about Jeff and Sheri. That he needed her help. He was honest enough to admit the teenagers didn't have a thing to do with it.

He'd called her house; Sheri had informed him that Alice had gone to A Coffee and Pastry Place to visit with her foster mother. So, like some infatuated adolescent, here he was.

Hayes frowned and started across the narrow, tree-lined parking lot. Had he come for forgiveness? Some sort of absolution?

If so, this would be the place to put their ghosts to rest. They'd met here. He'd been a fledgling lawyer, still reeling from his wife's death, overwhelmed with the prospect of being a single parent. She had been a college freshman, home for summer break, working here at her foster mother's coffeehouse. She'd been bursting with enthusiasm for life, excitement at facing the future, with idealism.

One night business had been particularly slow, and she'd done what he'd kept himself from doing for weeks—started a conversation. She'd asked what he was reading, then laughed when he'd told her. *"Proust?"* *she'd repeated. "Lighten up, reading's supposed to be fun."* He'd taken her suggestion, and the next time he'd come in, they'd had a lively discussion about Stephen King's ability to scare the socks off even the most jaded of readers.

One thing had led to another.

Hayes shook his head and climbed the raised cottage's front steps and crossed the porch. It seemed so obvious to him now why he'd been drawn to her, considering what had been going on in his life. He'd fed on her energy, her enthusiasm and idealism. She'd filled an empty space inside him, a place that had ached to be filled.

A place that still ached.

Ridiculous.

Scowling, Hayes pushed that thought away and entered the coffeehouse. Although crowded, he spotted

Alice immediately. She sat at a corner table, her dark head bent over an opened newspaper. As he watched, she reached up to tuck her hair behind her ear. It refused to be anchored, and feathered over her cheek once more.

The simple gesture transported him back twelve years. She'd done the same thing, with the same results, hundreds of times before. Sometimes he would beat her to it and tuck the hair behind her ear himself. It behaved no better for him than her.

Smiling to himself, he walked over to her. "Hello, Alice."

She lifted her head and met his eyes. In hers he read the barest hint of vulnerability. Of trepidation. Both served to remind him how much time had passed. Twelve years ago he would have seen expectation in her eyes. And pleasure.

The realization left him feeling bereft.

"Hayes," she murmured, folding her hands on top of the newspaper.

He moved his gaze over her upturned face, her warm brown eyes and full mouth, her small straight nose and smooth soft skin. His chest tightened. She was still the most beautiful woman he had ever known. "What are you reading?"

She hesitated, then lowered her eyes to the paper. "About the boy in Florida who divorced his parents."

He made a face. "Lighten up. Reading's supposed to be fun."

"We've played this scene before."

"It's a rerun. And during sweeps week at that."

A smile pulled at her mouth, and he had a sense that she couldn't help herself.

"Got a suggestion?"

"Uh-huh." He reached around her and flipped through the paper until he found the funnies. "There you go."

She lowered her eyes, then lifted them back to his, hers alight with humor. "The entire page, or one strip in particular?"

"I'm partial to Doonesbury or Drabble. But you might take a look at Cathy." He motioned the chair across from hers. "May I join you?"

Alice hesitated a moment, then shook her head. "I don't think that would be a good idea."

"You don't?"

"You here for a reason, Hayes?"

"To see you."

"Really?" She dropped her hands to her lap. "I can't imagine why. We pretty much said everything there was to say to each other the other night."

"Did we?"

She narrowed her eyes. "Stop that. I hate when you do that."

He slipped uninvited into the chair opposite her, smiling at the way she gritted her teeth. "When I do what?"

"I'm the therapist here—okay, Hayes? I know all about leading questions. And I'm not biting." She arched an eyebrow with a cool arrogance she wouldn't have been able to manage at nineteen. "If there's nothing else, I have things to do."

He eyed the *Times Picayune*. "I see that."

"I'm visiting with Maggie."

He turned his gaze to the service counter and the line of customers, then met her eyes once more. "That's going to be kind of tough, at least for a while."

Alice sighed impatiently. "Oh, all right, you've got me, Counselor. I'm all ears. To what do I owe the annoyance of this visit?"

Hayes lowered his gaze to his hands. He cleared his throat and met her eyes. "Jeff. And Sheri. Of course."

"Of course," she repeated, disappointment moving through her. She called herself a fool. "That is the reason we're speaking after twelve years."

Something flickered across his expression, then was gone. "Thanks for the other night. For trying to smooth things between me and Jeff. And for helping him. He came home calmer. Less angry."

Alice shifted her gaze, uncomfortable with his sincerity. With the need she saw in his eyes. It called to her, reminded her of all the reasons they had become involved in the first place. And right now, she didn't want to be reminded of the past, of their months together. The memories were all around her, calling to her. And she was uncertain that she was strong enough to resist them.

"It's my job to help people become less angry," she said softly. "I'm good at it."

"If it were just doing your job, Sheri Kane wouldn't be occupying your guest bedroom. You have a big heart, Alice Dougherty."

She swallowed past the lump in her throat. Sometimes too big. So big she took in coldhearted cynics with eyes that told her things he didn't even believe. "I care about her. And Jeff."

"I do, too."

Alice drew in a deep, careful breath. "So, what do you suggest they do about the baby?"

He paused. "In my opinion, they're too young to get married. And I'm not a fan of abortion, legal or not."

"That leaves adoption."

"Yes."

Alice shifted her gaze to Maggie. She stood behind the counter, chatting with customers as she rang up their tabs. Maggie Ryan Adler was the kindest, most loving person Alice had ever known. Maggie had taken her off the streets and into her home, had been interested in her when no one else had cared, had given her love and respect when she'd never known anything but abuse and neglect.

Alice tilted her head. She often wondered what would have become of her without Maggie's kindness, without her love.

Hayes followed her gaze. "Maggie's children are adopted, aren't they?"

"Amanda and Josh. Yes." She smiled, thinking of the youngsters, of watching them grow and flourish. There had been so much love in that home, such a feeling of security and safety. It was what she had wanted for her own child, the one who had never been born.

Alice blinked against the tears that pricked at her eyes. "Maggie herself is adopted. Did you know that?" she asked, without shifting her gaze from her foster mother.

"No."

"Her situation was similar to mine. Abusive alcoholic parents. Only she escaped at a much younger age. Five, I think."

Maggie looked her way and smiled. Alice returned her smile, feeling filled suddenly with light and warmth. She turned back to Hayes. "Adoption is a wonderful option. I feel very strongly about it."

"I do, too." He folded his hands on the table in front of him. "I'll help any way I can."

"Sheri doesn't have any insurance. Right now she's going to the free clinic."

"No problem."

"The kids will have to agree." Alice shook her head. "And I'm not sure about Sheri. She really wants this baby."

"Doesn't she understand what her life will be like if she keeps the baby and tries to raise it on her own?" Hayes frowned. "Doesn't she see how much better off the baby would be with two stable parents? Parents who are grown-ups?"

"Of course not, Hayes. She's seventeen."

"You could talk to her."

"But I won't pressure her." At Hayes's frustrated expression, she caught his hands across the table. "You have to understand Sheri to understand why this baby is so important to her. She's never been loved, not really. She's never had someone to call her own. She wants both. More than anything in the world."

Alice squeezed his fingers, tears pricking at the back of her eyes once more, memories swamping her. Memories of how she'd felt when she'd learned of her own pregnancy. Memories of her own needs. Her own hopes and dreams. "She knows this baby will love her. Unconditionally. And Sheri knows this baby will let her love her back. No one has ever allowed Sheri to love them."

For a long moment, Hayes was silent. He met her eyes, the expression in his soft with compassion. "You understand her so well because she's like you."

Alice's breath caught. She didn't need his pity. She didn't want it. She tried to free her hands, but he held on to them. "Is that the way you felt, Alice? About our child?"

And about you. And Jeff. She squeezed her eyes shut, recalling her dizzying hope and happiness, then her utter despair. In one fell swoop, she had lost everything.

"Is it, Alice?"

She opened her eyes; she knew they were glassy with tears. "Yes."

"I'm sorry, Alice. I'm so sorry." He moved his fingers over her hands, stroking, caressing. "I didn't realize. I didn't know how much... the baby meant to you."

It took a moment for his words, their meaning, to sink in, but when they did anger took her breath. "Because it meant nothing to you! When I got pregnant, all you felt was trapped. You agreed to marry me because that was the honorable and manly thing to do. But you never wanted me and you never wanted our baby." She yanked her hands from his grasp and stood. "Now, excuse me. I have things to do."

Tears flooding her eyes, she started for the door, moving blindly between the tables and patrons, praying she could keep from humiliating herself until she made it outside.

She cleared the front door, and the tears spilled over. The cold stung her wet cheeks, and she realized she'd left her sweater inside. She'd sooner die than go back for it and have Hayes see her this way, she thought. Maggie would save it for her.

Hugging herself, she hurried across the porch and down the steps to the parking lot. She reached her car and fumbled in her purse for the keys, coming up empty-handed.

Her keys were in her sweater pocket. Damn.

She sagged against the car. She couldn't go back in there. She couldn't face Hayes. She—

"You forgot this."

He'd followed her. Alice brushed the tears from her cheeks, then turned. She took the sweater from his outstretched hand, not meeting his eyes. She didn't think she could bear to see the pity in them.

"Thanks," she murmured, her voice still thick with tears. She dipped her fingers into the pocket, found her keys and pulled them out. "I guess I'd better—"

He covered her hand with his. "I'm sorry, Alice."

"Our relationship didn't work out," she said stiffly. "That's life. There's nothing for you to be sorry about. I don't want your apologies or your pity." She slipped her hand from his. "Just leave me alone."

"I wasn't referring to our relationship." He turned her gently to face him. "I'm sorry we lost the baby."

She drew in a shuddering breath, her eyes welling with tears again. She fought them spilling over. "Right. I really believe that, Hayes."

"You should. Because I am truly sorry." He slid his hands up to her shoulders. "I didn't want the baby the same way you did. I couldn't, don't you see? We were so different, and at such different places in our lives. But the baby was mine. Ours. It was alive, growing. A part of my life already, even if only for a few months."

Alice battled to breathe evenly. The pain balled in her chest, her throat. Twelve years ago they'd hardly spoken about the miscarriage; now, all these years later, it felt as if it had just happened. As if she were alone in that antiseptic hospital room, stripped bare of all her dreams.

"It...hurt...so much."

Her breath caught on a sob, and he drew her against his chest. "I know, sweetheart. I know now."

She slipped her arms around him, holding tightly, sobbing against his shoulder. "I wanted her more than...anything. She was mine. She was inside me. Growing. A part of me."

For a long time she cried, until she didn't have any tears left. But still he held her, murmuring sounds of comfort, gently rocking. The heat of his body warmed her. The scent of him seeped into her consciousness until it filled her senses. Beneath her hands, she became aware of the feel of him, hard and strong and male.

Her hurt and despair lessened, then disappeared altogether. Awareness replaced them.

She pressed her face into the crook of his neck, breathing deeply. His five o'clock shadow was rough against her cheek; his skin was warm and smelled of soap and sweat.

She squeezed her eyes shut. She'd missed this—him—so much. She'd missed his arms, his touch. She had missed the way his arms had made her feel—desired and womanly, safe.

No other man had been able to make her feel the same way. No man ever would. She'd finally stopped looking.

Alice tipped her head back and met his eyes. In them she saw her awareness mirrored back at her. A shudder moved over her, and she pressed her hands against his chest. "This is a mistake. We both know it."

"Yes," he murmured, tightening his arms around her, his voice thick. "A mistake."

She slid her hands to his shoulders and tipped her face more fully to his. "I should go."

"Yes," he murmured again, lowering his mouth. "Go. Now."

She ordered herself to do just that; she parted her lips instead. He caught her mouth, then her tongue. She made a sound of pleasure deep in her throat, and the car keys slipped from her fingers.

He tasted familiar, she thought dizzily. Smelled familiar. Rich and male. She recognized the way he moved his mouth against hers. The way he flattened his hands against her lower back and held her to him. Firmly. Possessively.

She wound her fingers in his hair, urging him to deepen the kiss. To take more. To bring her closer. Kissing Hayes felt like coming home.

With a muffled oath, Hayes pulled away. He met her eyes, his dark with arousal, his expression stunned. She parted her lips to speak; before she could, he lowered his mouth once more, capturing hers.

This time he plundered. Demanded. This time he took her mouth with a fury born of years of denial. She answered his passion with her own. Standing on tiptoes, she pressed herself against him, digging her fingers in his hair, pulling him closer, straining against him.

She felt his arousal in the way he held her, the way he plunged his fingers into her hair, cupping the back of her head to anchor her to him. She felt it in the way he rasped her name, as if it came from a dark and desperate place inside him, in the way he greedily devoured her lips.

Alice made a sound of pleasure deep in her throat, reveling in the knowledge of how strongly she affected him. He affected her just as strongly. For as close as they were, she wanted him closer still. She wanted his hands on her, wanted his naked flesh pressed to hers.

When had awareness become arousal, overpowering and insistent? When had she decided to give herself to Hayes, body and soul? Twelve years ago, she thought dizzily. In all that time, nothing had changed. She still wanted him with a ferocity that stole her good sense, her ability to reason, everything but her desire to be with him.

Hayes tore his mouth from hers, breathing hard. She saw the regret in his eyes. The apology. Shame hit her in a wave. As did hurt. Once again, she had opened the door for Hayes to hurt her.

Furious, with herself, with him, she struggled against his grasp. He tightened his arms, and she swore. "Let me go, Hayes. Damn you, let me go."

"You never lacked, Alice," he said fiercely. "Never. Letting you go was hell, but it was for the best."

She stopped struggling and stared at him, stunned. He was convincing her. Trying to make her "see" so she wouldn't be angry. She jerked out of his arms. "You bastard. You didn't come here tonight to talk about Sheri and Jeff, did you?"

"No."

She balled her hands into fists on his chest. "You couldn't leave it alone, could you? You can't stand for anyone to have a different opinion than yours."

"That's not true." She made a move to duck past him; he caught her hand. "I didn't come here tonight to try to convince you of anything. I came because I couldn't stay away."

And he hated that. She saw that truth. He saw wanting her as a weakness. A mistake.

She'd always wanted him more than he'd wanted her. He'd proved that twelve years ago when he'd rejected her flatly. And here she stood, offering him the same opportunity. When was she going to stop allowing this man to hurt her? When was she going to stop wearing her heart on her sleeve for him to crush?

Now, she decided. Tilting her head back, she met his eyes. "Let me go, Hayes. This moment."

"Alice—"

"Now."

He dropped his hands and stepped away from her. "I don't know what to say to you. What do you want me to say?"

"That's just it. I don't want you to say anything." Bending, she scooped up her car keys. She jammed the key into the door lock and twisted. Swinging the door open, she forced him to step back.

She slid behind the wheel and started the car, then looked back up at him. "Do me a favor, Hayes. Next time you're trying to stay away, try a little harder."

Chapter Five

Alice let herself into her house, hands shaking so badly she had difficulty fitting the key into the lock. Once inside, she shut the door and leaned against it, grateful for its support. Dear Lord, what had she been thinking? She'd long ago learned her lesson with Hayes; only a fool made the same mistake twice.

Then she was the biggest fool of all. For tonight she'd fallen into Hayes's arms as easily, and as passionately, as she had at nineteen.

She might never be the same again.

Sheri appeared in the kitchen doorway, a plate of Oreo cookies in one hand, a glass of milk in the other. She smiled. "Hey, Miss A."

"Hey," Alice repeated weakly, and motioned at the plate of cookies. "I hope that's not your dinner."

"Nope. I had a peanut butter sandwich and an apple a couple of hours ago." The teenager cocked her head and frowned. "You all right, Miss A.?"

Alice forced a stiff smile. "Fine, Sheri. Just tired."

Sheri looked unconvinced. "Jeff's dad called. He was looking for you, so I told him where you were. I hope that was okay?"

"Fine." Alice slipped out of her sweater. "He stopped by the coffeehouse. No big deal."

Sheri frowned and shifted her weight from one foot to the other. "What did he want?"

What had Hayes wanted? She knew what she'd wanted: to make love. For those few dizzying moments in the parking lot she had wanted that desperately. Shamelessly, even. The memory of those moments filled her head—Hayes's mouth on hers, demanding, exploring; his taste on her tongue; the feel of him under her hands, hard and hungry; their bodies pressed together, hot with arousal.

Alice brought her hand to her mouth. She caught herself and swore silently. If only her lips didn't still burn from Hayes's kiss. If only she could forget the way she'd felt in his arms—as if she would die if he stopped touching her. If only she could block out the way she'd reacted to him—as though she were starving for sex, starving for him.

"Miss A.?"

Alice glanced at Sheri, then away quickly. Her cheeks, she knew, were bright with color; she felt as transparent as a picture window. How would Sheri react if she knew the truth?

Alice cleared her throat. "He didn't want anything. He just...stopped by." She crossed to the hall closet, hung up her sweater, then made a great show of yawning. "I think I'll turn in early and read for a while."

"Oh . . . okay."

Sheri gazed at the floor a moment, and Alice sensed the girl's hesitation, her need to say something. Alice didn't give her the opportunity—she couldn't deal with anyone but herself tonight, couldn't deal with anyone's else's troubles or confusion. She had her own to handle. And truthfully, as emotionally raw as she felt at this moment, she wasn't certain she could even deal with her own.

"Good night, Sheri." Alice forced a smile and started for her room, anxious to be alone.

"Miss A.?"

Alice stopped and glanced over her shoulder; the teenager hadn't moved. "Yes, Sheri?"

The girl caught her bottom lip between her teeth, then shook her head. "Nothing. I...I put the mail on the kitchen table. That's all."

Alice smiled again. "Thanks. I think I'll take a look at it."

After wishing Sheri a good-night, Alice headed to the kitchen. There, as Sheri had promised, the mail sat in a neat stack in the middle of the table. She picked up the stack and sifted through it. Included with the usual assortment of bills and advertisements was a letter hand-addressed to her with a local postmark but no return address.

Curious, she slit open the envelope, pulled out the single sheet of loose leaf paper and scanned it, her hands beginning to shake.

Her mother. It couldn't be.

Alice's knees gave and she sank onto one of the kitchen chairs. She stared down at the note, stunned.

How had her mother found her? How had she—
Mrs. Schultz. That's right. Alice pressed the heels
of her hands to her eyes. She'd run into the woman, a
neighbor from her childhood, several months back.

Alice remembered being uncomfortable with the
woman's questions, remembered trying to be vague
about where she lived, about what she was doing now.
Not that she had ever worried about hiding her
whereabouts. After all, her mother had never wanted
her, never tried to contact her.

Until now.

Alice closed her eyes and tried to picture her mother's face, but couldn't. Instead she saw Maggie's dark
hair and eyes, Maggie's smile, heard Maggie's musi-
cal laughter and kind voice.

*She couldn't remember what her mother looked
like.*

Alice caught her breath, a strange sensation moving over her. A sensation that left her feeling anxious,
panicky, even. She didn't want to see her mother. She
didn't want to remember what her mother looked like.
For fifteen years she had been able to pretend her biological mother and father didn't exist. That her pre-
vious life didn't exist. She liked it that way; she didn't
want it to change.

Alice lowered her eyes to the letter once more. Her
father was dead. Since last month. Drunk, he'd fallen
down a flight of stairs and broken his neck.

Dead. Her father was dead. Alice closed her eyes
and tried to sort through the emotions barreling
through her. How did she feel about her father's
death? He'd been her father, after all. His seed had
given her life. He should have been one of the most
important people in her life.

Instead she didn't feel anything. Not regret or remorse, not even relief. She felt nothing.

Now her mother wanted to be a family with her daughter again. She wanted to pick up where they had left off.

A family.

Alice squeezed her eyes shut, emotion choking her, her memory winging her back to her childhood, to the frightened, inadequate girl she had been. She'd never been able to do anything right. Had never been the child her parents wanted. She'd tried so hard to please them. To be deserving of their love and affection.

She'd failed every time.

A tear slipped from the corner of an eye and rolled down her cheek. She swiped at it, but another followed, then another. Why hadn't her mother wanted to be a family before? Why hadn't her parents loved her?

Memories flooded her mind. Of her mother, drunk, berating her for being lazy and stupid, her mother flinging a beer bottle at her.

Alice rubbed her shoulder, rubbed the scar she carried to remind her of the incident, her mind shifting to memories of her father. Beating her for being useless, for being underfoot when he wanted her gone. And when she was older, her father putting his hands on her, trying to touch her in places a father should never touch.

A sob rose in her throat, the bile of revulsion with it. She'd fought him off and taken shelter on the street. Maggie had found and saved her.

Now, her mother wanted them to be a family?

Alice crumpled the letter. She didn't want to see her mother. She didn't want to remember. She'd left that life, that frightened girl, far behind. It had been her parents who had been lacking, not her.

Then why did she feel as if she were ten years old and worthless?

"Miss A.? Are you all right?"

Alice looked up to find Sheri standing in the doorway, her expression stricken. Alice opened her mouth to reassure the teenager, but found she could not. She gazed helplessly at the girl, tears spilling over, rolling down her cheeks.

"Is it something I did?" Sheri whispered, moving haltingly into the room. "If it is, I'm sorry. I wouldn't hurt you for anything."

The innocent always blamed themselves.

Alice shook her head, the tears coming harder. She wanted to smile, to assure the youngster that everything was fine. But her tears refused to be quelled.

"Oh, Miss A. Please don't cry." Sheri crossed the room and dropped down beside her, beginning to cry herself. Curving her arms around Alice, she laid her head in her lap. "It's going to be all right. I know it is."

Alice bent and laid her head against Sheri's. "You sound like me," she murmured, her words strangled with tears.

"Then you should listen. You're a really smart lady."

Alice smiled weakly and feathered her fingers through the teenager's cap of silky dark hair. "I didn't mean to upset you."

The teenager made a sound that was a cross between a sniffle and a giggle. "That's okay. It's not your fault. I'm kind of emotional these days."

"I remember what it was like."

As soon as the words passed her lips she realized her mistake. She'd never talked about her pregnancy with anyone but Hayes and Maggie.

Sheri tilted her head back. "What do you mean, Miss A.? Did you have a baby?"

Alice wiped the tears from her cheeks. "No, I never had a baby. I was pregnant once, though."

"What happened?"

Alice hesitated, not wanting to upset the teenager, but knowing she had to tell her the truth. "I...lost her. I was about three months along."

Fear flew into Sheri's eyes. "You don't...think that I...you know, that I could..." Her throat closed over the words.

Alice tapped the end of Sheri's nose with her index finger. "No, I don't."

"But..." Sheri drew her eyebrows together. "What happened? Why did you...lose it?"

"I don't know why. I just did. I didn't have any warning. I guess it just...wasn't meant to be."

Sheri was quiet a moment, as if contemplating Alice's words. "How did you feel after? I mean, how did you face it?"

I felt like I wanted to die. Tears flooded her eyes. "I was brokenhearted. But I—" She lifted her shoulders. "I had to go on."

"You've done a lot of that, haven't you, Miss A.? Going on, I mean."

The teenager's words caught her unaware, touching a core place inside her. Alice's gaze moved unwittingly to her mother's letter, lying crumpled on the floor by their feet. "Yeah," she murmured. "But then, I think we all do."

* * *

Although Alice had tossed her mother's letter in the trash and told herself that the past could only touch her if she let it, she couldn't shake the way receiving the letter had made her feel. Uncertain and anxious. Vulnerable.

She'd found herself walking on tenterhooks the next few days, worried that her mother might try to call her or stop by, and a knot formed in her stomach every time she saw the stack of mail waiting on the kitchen table for her.

Sighing, she rested her head against the couch back. Outside, a spring storm raged. Rain beat against her roof and windows; lightning flashed across the black sky. She turned her gaze from the window and sighed again. She despised feeling this way—off-kilter and out of sorts. Years ago she'd taken charge of her life and had never looked back. Now, between her mother and Hayes, she was being forced to look back.

Hayes.

Alice brought a hand to her mouth and ran her fingers gently across her lips. She hadn't spoken to him since the night at the coffeehouse, yet she'd been unable to put him out of her mind. Had he thought of her? she wondered. Had those minutes in the coffeehouse parking lot been as tumultuous for him as they had been for her?

She made a sound of self-derision. Right. Would she ever stop playing the fool for Hayes Bradford?

Thunder shook the old house, and Alice jumped as she realized someone was pounding on the front door. She checked her watch and frowned. Nearly eleven. Who would call so late? And on a work night, no less. She thought of Tim Benson, of her meeting with him that morning, of his expression when she and Dennis had asked him, as gently as possible, to leave the program. She shivered. In that moment she had understood why Sheri felt so uncomfortable around the boy. Something in his eyes had made her feel threatened.

The pounding came again, and she stood and walked cautiously to the door. She inched aside one of the sidelight's lace sheers. Hayes stood on her porch, soaked to the skin, his hair slicked to his head. She quickly unlocked the door and opened it.

"Hayes? What are you—"

"Is he here?"

Alice didn't have to ask whom he meant. His panicked expression said it all. She shook her head. "I'm sorry, Hayes. I haven't seen him."

He sighed in frustration and ran a hand through his dripping hair. "Is Sheri?"

Alice nodded and motioned behind her. "She went to bed early. She wasn't feeling well."

"I hate to ask, Alice, but is she alone?"

"Yes, of course. She—" Alice hesitated, remembering the night Sheri had let Jeff crawl in her window. "At least, I think she is."

"Would you check? Please?"

Shivering, Alice nodded and stepped away from the door. "Come in. I'll get you a towel."

She got the towel for Hayes, then went to check on Sheri. She eased the bedroom door open a crack and peeked inside. The girl was curled up on her side, deeply asleep. And obviously alone. Alice scanned the rest of the room, finding it empty.

She breathed a silent sigh of relief. She would have hated it if she'd found that Sheri had violated her trust by hiding Jeff in her room a second time.

Alice rejoined Hayes in the foyer. "Sorry," she murmured, "Sheri's alone. And as far as I know, they didn't speak tonight. The phone didn't ring, anyway."

Hayes rubbed the bridge of his nose. "Great, I don't know where else to look for him. I called all the family, his friends, even his baseball coach."

Alice's heart went out to him. He looked exhausted. The lines in his face seemed more deeply etched tonight, his eyes shadowed with fatigue and worry. She longed to reach out and smooth those lines, to offer comfort and reassurance. She called herself a fool.

"Could I use your phone? Maybe he's home now."

"Sure. It's by the sofa." She motioned toward the kitchen. "I was having cocoa. I'll bring you a cup."

He hesitated, moving his eyes over her. "Are you sure? It looks as if I've kept you up already."

Alice glanced down at herself, remembering for the first time that she wore her bedclothes. Heat washed over her, even as she called herself a ninny. Her robe concealed more than many of her day clothes.

"I wasn't sleeping," she murmured, automatically tightening the robe's cinch belt. "You won't be keeping me up—you'll be keeping me company. Go on in. I'll bring the cocoa."

When she returned to the living room with the steaming mug, she found that Hayes had already positioned himself on the floor. He'd removed his shoes, socks and jacket; it looked as if he'd towel-dried and finger-combed his hair. He leaned against the sofa, his eyes closed.

Her chest tight, she used the moment to gaze at him. She'd always liked looking at him, had always thought him the most handsome man in the world. And looking at him had always made her feel warm and fluttery inside.

Silly, she thought, moving her gaze down his lean body. She'd always been just little bit silly when it had come to Hayes Bradford. No surprises tonight; she felt warm and fluttery and just about as silly as a woman could be over a man.

She drew in a deep, shuddering breath, working to even her runaway pulse. Why did he affect her this way? How could nothing more than his presence turn her to mush? And why did his sitting on the floor in her living room feel so right?

He opened his eyes and met hers. For one long moment he simply looked at her intently, unsmiling. A flutter of awareness moved over her, and she acknowledged that inviting him for cocoa had been a poor decision indeed. The hour was late, the setting too intimate. And she was way too susceptible to Hayes Bradford's brand of charm.

She forced a bright smile, although she suspected he could see right through it. "Here you go." She bent and held out the mug. He took it, his fingers brushing hers, his gaze sliding to the gaping V of her robe. Heat washed over her once more, and she started to straighten.

He reached up and caught her hand. "Don't go, Alice."

"I'm not going anywhere."

"But you are. You're headed clear across the room to that uncomfortable understuffed chair." He indicated a place on the floor beside him. "Sit by me."

She hesitated, and he smiled. "I won't bite." He lifted two fingers. "Scout's honor." She hesitated only a moment more, then sat beside him. Their shoulders almost touched, and the heat from his body made her too warm, even in her light robe.

She brought her mug to her lips. She never had been able to resist even his simplest requests. *A fool. She was such a fool.*

For long moments they stared at nothing in particular, the room silent save for the sound of the rain and the occasional boom of thunder.

"We fought again," Hayes said finally, quietly, his voice heavy with regret. "He stormed off."

"I figured that was what must have happened." She laced her fingers around the warm mug. "How long ago?"

Hayes made a sound of frustration. Of worry. "Hours."

"And you've checked everywhere?"

"Yes." He drew his eyebrows together. "All I can do now is wait. I don't think I have another option. I left a message for him to call me here when he returns." Hayes lowered his eyes to his cup. "I brought up the idea of adoption. I pushed too hard." He laughed, the sound hard and self-mocking. "You know me, Mr. Subtle."

She reached over and lightly touched his sleeve. "I'm sorry, Hayes."

He looked at her hand, then lifted his gaze to hers. "I appreciate that, Alice. You could have told me to take a flying leap. I wouldn't have blamed you if you had."

She drew her hand back. "But that's not my way."

"No, it's not." He met her eyes, searching, studying. "What about you? It's late." He lifted the mug. "You're indulging in cocoa. What ails you tonight?"

"I couldn't sleep. Too much on my mind." She leaned her head against the edge of the couch. "I had to expel one of my kids from the program today."

"Had to?"

"I recommended it, but..."

"But you hated to do it."

"Yes. He needs us. He needs help." She ran her fingers back and forth across the rug, creating broken, ragged shapes in the pile. "But he needs it from a different kind of program. We weren't doing him any good."

"You feel like you failed him."

"I did fail him." She sighed and swiped her hand across the marks on the rug, obliterating them. "He's back on drugs. Still angry at the world. In truth, he's no better off than when he started in the program a year ago."

Hayes caught her hand, closing his fingers over hers. "You can't save everybody, Alice."

She looked down at their joined hands, then back at him. She shook her head. "I don't believe that. I keep thinking that if I'd only tried harder, I'd have found a way to reach him."

"Some people don't want to be saved."

She couldn't argue with him; she knew what he said was true. But it frustrated the hell out of her. She didn't want to let even one of her kids go.

She slipped her hand from his. "Would you like another cup of—"

"I'm fine. I haven't finished what I have." Hayes picked up his cup and sipped, licking his lips appreciatively as he did. "I haven't had a cup of cocoa in years." He smiled in wry amusement. "You used to make it all the time," he murmured. "Even in August."

She looked away, remembering all the times she'd made the three of them a cup of the hot, sweet beverage. "You always seemed to like it."

He met her eyes. "And I always liked this, Alice. Being with you. Just sitting. Enjoying the quiet."

What could she say? she wondered, swallowing hard. And even if she could find a thought, how could she verbalize it—her chest ached so badly she could hardly breathe, let alone speak.

"I missed it when you were gone."

She tightened her fingers on the ceramic mug. "But you were the one who sent me away. The one who ended it."

His lips twisted, and he shifted his gaze to the dark, rain-splattered windows. "I know."

"Then why are you telling me, Hayes? It's over. Is there something you want me to say? Something you want me to feel?"

He frowned, his gaze still on the windows. "I don't...want anything from you, Alice. I just wanted you to know." He met her eyes then, the expression in his tearing at her. "You were important to me. You were special."

She curled her fingers into fists. *But not important enough. Not special enough.* Disappointment and frustration welled in her chest, until she could taste them.

A brilliant flash of lightning illuminated the already warmly lit room. She faced him, her heart rapping furiously against the wall of her chest. "I think it's time for you to go."

"I'd rather stay."

"Sorry." She started to stand; he caught her hand and pulled her back down.

"I always thought you the most beautiful woman I'd ever known," he murmured, running his fingers over hers, dipping them in the junctures of hers.

She shook her head, her mouth desert dry. Warmth radiated from where his fingers covered hers, upward and outward until her entire body felt aflame. "I'm not beautiful. Not by any stretch of the imagination."

"By mine you are." He laid her hand against his chest, over his thundering heart. "The most beautiful."

She sucked in a quick, desperate breath. She felt her control evaporating, her resolve melting away. She tried to pull back, but he tightened his grasp. "Don't do this, Hayes."

"Don't do what?"

"Turn me inside out," she whispered. "Make me crazy to kiss you."

"Are you?" He drew her a fraction closer. "Crazy to kiss me?"

"Yes, dammit." She tugged on her hand. "Now, let me go."

Instead, with a quick jerk, he tumbled her against him, then brought her backward with him until she lay sprawled across his chest.

"You make me crazy, too," he said softly. "You turn me inside out. And upside down. And backward." He eased his hands down her back to the curve of her bottom. He pressed her against him. "See how crazy you make me? And you do it effortlessly. All I have to do is think of you. Look at you. Touch you."

The breath shuddered past her lips, arousal licking at the last of her control, her resolve long gone already. "Hayes...this isn't—"

What could she say? That this wasn't right? Nothing had felt so right in a long time. That she didn't want him? What a joke. She wanted him so badly she thought she might die if she didn't have him.

He rolled her onto her back and propped himself above her. "I can't sleep, Alice. I can't concentrate on work. My relationship with my son is unraveling at the speed of light, and yet...all I can think about is being with you."

Hayes trailed his mouth across her eyebrow, down the curve of her cheek. He found the pulse that beat behind her ear, and he pressed a kiss to the spot. "I never forgot what it was like being with you. And I won't apologize for wanting you. I can't. It's been the one thing in the course of my life that's felt totally right."

He moved his mouth lower, to the base of her throat. She whimpered and arched. "You feel like silk and you taste like sugar." He moved his mouth again, lower, nudging aside the soft terry cloth, revealing the curve of her breast. Heat spiraled through her as he sampled that spot, then moved to another. Then another. Stroking, tasting. Nipping.

Alice raised her hands to his hair. "You said you wouldn't bite," she whispered brokenly. "You promised. Scout's honor."

He brought his face back to hers. "Yeah, but I was never a Scout."

Giving in to the sensations coursing through her, she brought his mouth to hers. He tasted of the chocolate, rich and sweet. He smelled of the storm, of the rainwater and sweat. And he felt like Hayes. Solid and strong.

With a sigh, she twined her fingers in his hair. She remembered everything about his kiss, his touch, his lovemaking. The way he held his head, the exact amount of pressure; the way he moved his lips against hers; the sounds he made, deep and raspy, as she responded to his loving. It felt so right, so familiar.

It felt like coming home.

"Miss A.! Where are you? I don't feel so good!"

Sheri's words sliced through the fog of pleasure that enveloped her, and Alice rolled away from Hayes. She scrambled to her feet, automatically adjusting her robe, horrified at her wanton behavior. "I'm here, Sheri. What's wrong?"

Sheri stumbled into the living room, holding her middle, her face ashen. "I don't know...it hurts. And there was a...some spots of blood."

The baby. Oh, no. Alice's heart flew to her throat, but she managed to hide her fear. For Sheri's sake, she had to keep her head. "Calm down, sweetie." Alice went around the sofa and took the panicked girl's arm. "Come on, let's sit down."

Sheri clutched at her hand. "I don't want to lose my baby, Miss A. Don't let that happen! Please, don't...let..."

Her words trailed off as she saw Hayes for the first time. The blood drained from her already pale face. She shifted her gaze from Alice to Hayes and back, a look of shock crossing her features.

Alice dragged a hand through her tangled hair, imagining how she must appear, but too worried about Sheri to really care. "Hayes came searching for Jeff. We were having a cup of—"

"Jeff?" the girl squeaked, shifting her frightened gaze to Hayes. "Has something happened? Is something wrong—is he—"

"He's fine," Hayes interrupted quietly, obviously hearing the note of hysteria in the girl's voice and wanting to reassure her. "He left without telling me where he was going. I thought maybe he'd come here. That's all."

Alice shot Hayes an appreciative glance as she led Sheri to a chair. Beneath her hand, Alice could feel the girl tremble. She eased her onto the seat, then met her eyes. "I'm going to call Dr. Bennett."

The teenager caught her hand. "You think something's wrong, don't you?"

"Of course not." Alice squeezed Sheri's ice-cold fingers and forced a reassuring smile. "But we need to make sure. And you know Dr. Bennett. She'll have our heads if we don't call."

Sheri nodded miserably. "If you have to."

Alice called the doctor's service, and within minutes, Sheri's physician had returned her call. Alice quickly explained Sheri's symptoms, and the physician told them she had better examine the girl.

Heart thundering, Alice turned back to Sheri. She forced another calm smile. "Dr. Bennett thinks you should come in for an examination. She's going to meet us at the hospital."

"Hospital?" Sheri repeated, her chin wobbling, her eyes flooding with tears. "She thinks I'm...losing my baby, doesn't she?"

There was a chance. But how could she tell Sheri that? Alice took a deep breath. "It's a precaution. She doesn't want to take any chances, that's all. I'll get your robe and slippers—"

The phone rang, and Alice grabbed it, thinking it might be the doctor. It was Jeff; he'd returned home and found Hayes's message. Alice filled the boy in on what was going on, then handed the receiver to Sheri. While the teenagers talked, Alice retrieved the robe and slippers, quickly threw on street clothes then grabbed an afghan to wrap around Sheri.

She returned to the living room. Talking to Jeff had seemed to calm Sheri, and Alice said a silent thank-you. The calmer Sheri remained, the better. She knew that from experience.

"I'll go start the car," Hayes said suddenly, stiffly.

Alice turned to him. He stood as still as a stone, his expression almost forbidding. "That's not necessary," she said. "I can drive."

"Sheri may need you." Hayes slipped into his wet jacket. "I'll drive."

Unfortunately, Alice couldn't argue with that. "Okay, then. Let's go."

Chapter Six

The drive to the hospital took only a matter of minutes. Hayes navigated the slippery streets with a breathtaking combination of daring and caution. Save for Sheri's occasional whimper, they all remained silent.

Alice glanced at Hayes's profile, reflected in the rearview mirror. Even though she called herself an idiot, Alice couldn't help wondering what he was thinking. His expression told her nothing. His mouth was set in a grim, determined line; a muscle worked in his jaw.

Was he remembering, as she was, a night like this twelve years earlier? Only she'd been the one huddled under the blanket. She'd been the one whimpering with a combination of fear and pain.

She tore her gaze from his reflection, disappointment and hurt barreling over her. She thought not. He seemed as unaffected by this calamity as he'd been by theirs.

When they arrived at the hospital, Jeff was waiting just outside the emergency room's double-glass doors, his expression frantic with worry. When he saw Sheri, he raced to help her from the car, sparing only a fierce scowl for his father.

He cupped her face in his palms. "Sheri... sweetheart, are you all right?"

She threw her arms around him and clung to him, crying. "I'm so scared, Jeff. And I... it hurts."

"Don't worry, babe. It's going to be all right." Jeff's voice cracked, and he scooped Sheri into his arms and carried her inside.

Alice watched them, a lump in her throat. They really loved each other, she realized. It wasn't puppy love; it wasn't teen infatuation. They needed each other almost desperately; she saw that in the way they looked at and spoke to each other, in the way they clung to each other.

Did Hayes see it, too? she wondered, glancing at him from the corner of her eye. Hayes had been stoical with her, had tried to reason, to calm her with logic. He hadn't clung or cried or grieved. He hadn't promised to try to make everything all right, hadn't whispered reassurances about their having other babies.

Tears stung her eyes, and she blinked against them. Because there would be no other babies for them; no doubt he had already written her off.

Dr. Bennett arrived moments behind them and whisked Sheri into an examining room, leaving Jeff, Hayes and Alice to wait it out.

Hayes remained stiff and silent, doing no more than sending his son a visual reprimand and a slow-to-respond nurse a thunderous glance. He ignored Alice altogether and stood unmoving in front of the waiting-room window, staring out at the rain.

Alice couldn't stand still. She paced; she wrung her hands; she prayed for Sheri and Jeff and their unborn child. Jeff, too, couldn't remain still, and would slump in one of the vinyl chairs for a few moments, then jump up and nervously circle the room.

If only Hayes had cared that much about their baby, Alice thought, the tears tickling her eyes again. If only his ambivalence didn't still hurt so bad.

She balled her hands into fists. What had she been thinking tonight? Making out with Hayes like a nineteen-year-old who didn't know any better. She knew better. Her heart had the scars to prove it.

Dr. Bennett returned to the waiting room, all smiles. Although she'd determined there was no immediate danger, she prescribed quiet and bed rest for the next few days.

The trip home proved quieter than the trip to the emergency room. Jeff had asked his father, a bit belligerently, if he could accompany Sheri. To Hayes's credit, despite the late hour and Jeff's attitude, he had given his permission. Jeff had left his car at the hospital and the teenagers had sat in the back seat, cuddled together and whispering. She and Hayes had had nothing to say to each other.

Sheri and Jeff said good-night outside, then Alice helped the exhausted girl to her room. Alice tucked her into bed, adjusting the covers and pillows, fussing, she knew, like a mother hen. She couldn't help herself; she was so relieved that Sheri and her baby were all right.

"There you go," Alice said, smiling softly. "I want you to get some rest."

Sheri looked up at her, her eyes full of gratitude. "Thanks for being there for me, Miss A. I don't know what I would have done without you."

Alice brushed the hair gently away from Sheri's face. "I was happy to help. I'm just glad there's nothing wrong."

"Me, too." Sheri hesitated. "I was really scared, Miss A. I thought...you know, that what happened to you..."

"I know. But your baby is fine, so don't think about that anymore." Alice kissed her forehead, then flipped off the bedside light. "Get some sleep, sweetie. I'll be here if you need anything."

Sheri didn't respond and Alice thought her already asleep. She tiptoed to the door, stopping when Sheri murmured her name. Alice turned toward the girl, her heart doing a funny little flip at the sight of the teenager under the mountain of blankets. She looked so small and frail. She looked so young. "Yes, Sheri?"

"Jeff's dad...he's the one, isn't he?"

"The one who what?"

"The one who broke you heart."

Alice's chest tightened, and she struggled for a deep breath. "Yes," she whispered, "he's the one."

Sheri yawned and snuggled deeper under the covers. "I thought so. There's something about...the way...you...look at..."

Sheri words trailed off in sleep, and for long moments Alice stood at the bedroom door, gazing at the sleeping girl. Sheri's words ran crazily through her head, mocking her.

He's the one, isn't he? The one who broke your heart.

Why couldn't she remember that? Alice wondered, flexing her fingers. Was she some sort of a masochist? A glutton for punishment? He didn't love her. He never had. He'd hurt her so badly she'd thought she would never be whole again.

Alice shut Sheri's bedroom door. It had been difficult, but she had pieced her life back together. She had gone on. She would not allow Hayes back into her life or heart now; she would not give him the opportunity to hurt her again.

She turned and started toward the living room, stopping in surprise when she saw Hayes standing in the foyer. She started to shake. Tonight had brought back the fear and pain of her own miscarriage, the devastation of Hayes's rejection. And looking at him now was almost more than she could bear.

"You're still here," she said, working to mask her feelings.

"I wanted . . . to make sure she was okay."

"She is." Alice dragged a trembling hand through her hair, emotion and exhaustion pulling at her. "She's asleep already."

"She's lucky to have you."

"Actually, I think she's lucky to have Jeff."

Hayes searched her expression. "Maybe I'd better go."

"Yes." She folded her arms across her chest. "I think that's a good idea. Just go."

He took a step toward her instead. "Alice?"

She cocked her chin, cursing its wobble. "You're not leaving?"

"Is there . . . something wrong?"

"Should there be?"

He held his hands up. "If you want to play twenty questions and get nowhere, that's fine with me. I'm out of here." He started for the door.

"You wish Sheri had lost the baby. It would have solved your problem, wouldn't it?"

He stopped and turned slowly to face her. "That's nonsense."

"Just like my losing our baby solved your problem."

He stiffened. "You're tired and overwrought. Get some rest and in the morn—"

"Overwrought? I guess so." She heard the note of hysteria in her voice, felt the tug of exhaustion, and knew he was right. But no matter what she knew to be best, she couldn't leave well enough alone. "That's me, isn't it? Always overwrought."

He grasped the doorknob and twisted. "Now's not the time to discuss this, Alice. I'll call you tomorrow."

"It's never the time, is it?" She followed him to the door and, reaching around him, pushed it closed. "Did you mourn the loss of our baby? The other night you said you were sorry, but did you mourn her loss? Did you grieve even for a minute?"

"Alice—"

She balled her hands into fists on his chest. "Why didn't you comfort me? Would it have cost you so much to be kind?"

He covered her hands, holding them to his heart. Through his still-damp sweater she felt its runaway beat. "I didn't mean to be cruel," he said, his voice thick. "I tried to be strong for you. You were falling apart."

"I didn't need your strength, damn you. I needed you to understand." She drew in a shuddering breath. "I needed comfort. And love. Why couldn't you give me that? Did you despise me so much?"

"God, no! You think I would deliberately withhold something you needed? You think I would withhold—"

He dropped her hands and spun away from her. Through a haze of tears Alice gazed at his rigid back and shoulders.

"Don't you understand?" he said after a moment, so low she had to strain to hear. "I gave you everything I had. That's why..." He cleared his throat and turned back to her, the expression in his eyes bleak. "But everything I had wasn't enough or right. It never...would have been."

His words landed between them, plain, irrevocable. Familiar. She and Hayes weren't covering any new ground here, yet the words felt fresh. The wounds they inflicted felt new and bloody.

The pain twisted through her, tightening and taunting. She curved her arms around herself. "Don't call me, Hayes. Don't come to see me. It's over." She met his eyes. "It has been for a long time."

Getting through the next three days was hell. No matter how hard she tried, Alice hadn't been able to banish thoughts of Hayes from her mind. Alice shook her head as she climbed her porch steps. The minutes in his arms had been heaven; the ones after had been agony. Both continued to play in her head, stealing her sleep, her concentration, her peace of mind.

Every time she closed her eyes she saw him as he'd been the moment before he'd kissed her, then the moment she'd said goodbye.

With a frustrated shake of her head, she dug her keys out of her purse, unlocked the front door and stepped inside. "Sheri. I'm home."

Silence returned her greeting. Sheri had gone back to school today, although Alice had given her a stern lecture about taking it easy and resting as often as necessary if she became fatigued. The teenager hadn't experienced even a twinge of discomfort since the other night, and Dr. Bennett had given Sheri the okay to resume her regular activities—with moderation.

Alice slipped out of her sweater, tossed it across the back of a chair and headed for the kitchen. Sheri had been home from school; she'd stacked the day's mail in the middle of the table.

On top of the stack rested a hand-addressed plain white envelope. Alice gazed at it, knowing who'd sent it, a sick feeling in the pit of her stomach. Her mother had not taken her silence as a no.

Alice reached for the envelope, her hand beginning to shake. A part of her wanted to throw it out unopened. Pretend it didn't exist. She couldn't do that. She wasn't certain why, but she had to see the words her mother had written. Taking a deep breath, she picked up the envelope, tore it open and read its contents as quickly as possible.

Her mother had called repeatedly, hanging up when Alice answered the phone. She had come by the house, had stood on Alice's front porch, but had turned away without knocking.

With a sound of pain, Alice sank onto one of the kitchen chairs. She brought a shaking hand to her mouth. She thought of all the hang-up calls she'd gotten over the past few weeks, thought of the sensation she'd experienced when she'd received them—the sense that someone was hanging on the other end, listening, waiting.

Chill bumps raced up her arms. Had all the calls been from her mother? If not, which ones had been?

Alice rubbed her arms against the chill. Had Marge Dougherty recognized her daughter's voice? And if her mother had spoken, would she have recognized hers?

Oh, yes, Alice thought. Even after all the years that had passed, she would have recognized that hard, gravelly voice. It had been directed at her in anger too many times ever to forget.

Alice looked around her sunny kitchen, taking in the red-and-white tile counters and pine floor, the plant-lined window ledges, seeing them all as if for the first time. When had her mother stood on her front porch? Had she been home at the time? Had her mother caught a glimpse of her daughter through the window? Alice rubbed her arms again, shuddering. Her privacy had been violated, her space.

She felt as if she had been violated.

Alice lowered her eyes to the letter once more. Her mother was begging for another chance. *Begging*. She said she wanted desperately to make up for lost time.

Is that what they had lost? Alice wondered, tears rushing to her eyes. Time? The loss felt a lot more personal than that. A lot more . . . essential.

The letter blurred before her eyes. Had her mother changed? Had the years mellowed her? Is that why Marge Dougherty had come to her daughter's door and then turned away without knocking? The mother she'd known had been neither sensitive nor hesitant. She'd been bullish and sometimes brutal; she'd never held her feelings or opinions in check.

Alice swore and crumpled the letter. It didn't matter. She didn't want her mother back in her life; she wouldn't allow her back in. She'd buried the past, with its pain, fear and uncertainties, a long time ago.

Then why did she feel like a bad daughter, like a selfish and uncaring person?

Because a daughter was supposed to love her mother no matter what.

The tears flooded her eyes once more, this time trickling over. She swiped at her cheeks, angry with herself. Didn't that go both ways? Didn't a mother have a responsibility to be a good parent? To love and cherish and nurture?

Yes. For so many years she had longed for a sign of affection from her mother, for a scrap of love. But no more. Now she saw her mother for what she was. Now she knew that her mother had never been deserving of the love Alice had given her.

Alice sucked in a deep breath and stood. Crossing to the trash, she dropped the crumpled letter in. Her past was dead and buried.

From out front she heard the slam of a car door and voices raised in anger. She recognized Sheri's. Worried, she hurried toward the front door. Before she reached it, Sheri burst through. Jeff stood at the base of the porch steps, his expression stricken.

"I can't believe you said that!" Sheri cried, spinning to face the boy. "You don't love me. If you did you never could have suggested . . . that!"

"Sheri, wait!" Jeff bounded up the porch steps. "I do love you. You have to believe me. It's just—"

"Just what?" Her eyes flooded with tears. "Explain to me how giving our baby away shows how much you care about me!"

"If you'd just listen." He held his hand out. "Just let me try to explain."

"No! If you loved me you would..." She shook her head. "I shouldn't have to tell you what you would do if you loved me. Just go away! I never want to see you again. Never!"

Bursting into tears, the girl wheeled around and raced through the house. A moment later, Alice heard her bedroom door slam shut.

Alice turned back to Jeff, and her heart went out to him. He stood as if frozen by Sheri's words, his expression lost.

He turned his bleak gaze to her. "Can I go after her, Miss A.? Please? If I could just talk to her, I'm sure I could make her understand."

Alice hesitated, then shook her head. "I don't think so, Jeff. Not now, anyway. She seemed awfully upset already, and Dr. Bennett wanted her to take it easy." She sent him a reassuring smile. "But I'll talk to her, okay? Give her a couple of hours to calm down, then call."

He shifted his gaze from hers to the house beyond. His shoulders slumped. "I'm only trying to do the right thing." He dragged a hand through his hair, and Alice saw that it trembled. "How can she think I don't love her? I want what's best for us. All of us. And to be with her."

"I know, Jeff. And she does, too. This is a... hard time for her. Be patient, okay?"

He straightened his shoulders, visibly struggling to hide his feelings, to present a strong, manly front. In that instant he reminded her so much of Hayes that she ached.

"Sure." He shrugged and took a step back. "No problem."

"Thanks." Alice smiled. "You want me to tell her anything?"

"Tell her..." The words sounded choked, and he cleared his throat. "Tell her I love her. Okay?"

Tears stung Alice's eyes, and she nodded. "I will."

He turned, ran down the stairs and to his car. He slid behind the wheel, started and gunned the engine, then tore off.

Chest heavy and aching, Alice watched until he had disappeared from sight, then turned and went inside to comfort Alice. What was she going to say to the girl? From what she'd heard of their argument, she'd gleaned that Jeff had brought up the idea of adoption. Alice sighed. She had suspected Sheri would react to the idea this way. Twelve years ago she probably would have, too.

She stopped outside Sheri's bedroom door. From inside, she heard the girl's muffled sobs. Taking a deep breath, she knocked softly.

"Sheri, sweetie, it's me. May I come in?"

"Is he gone?"

Alice opened the door and stepped inside. Sheri lay across the bed on her stomach, her face buried in the pillows. "Yes. He was really upset, Sheri."

"Right." Sheri lifted her head. "He was upset."

Alice crossed to the old four-poster bed and sat on its edge. "Want to tell me what happened?"

"Sure you don't know already?"

Alice frowned, taken aback by the girl's sarcastic tone. "Other than what I assumed from your and Jeff's argument, yes, I'm sure I don't know."

Sheri pulled herself into a sitting position, scrunching a pillow to her middle. "Jeff thinks we... should—" Her eyes began to swim with tears. "He thinks we should...give our—" Her throat closed over the words, and she shook her head.

"Give your baby up for adoption," Alice said gently.

Sheri nodded, the tears beginning to slip down her cheeks. "How could he even...suggest that? If he really loved me, he couldn't. If he really loved me he would marry me."

Alice paused a moment to gather her thoughts. She couldn't avoid the truth just because Sheri wouldn't like it. She had a responsibility to both the teenagers. And she cared about them.

"You're not being fair to Jeff," she began. "Marriage, starting a family—those decisions are about more than love. They're about maturity and responsibility and—"

"I knew you'd say that!" Sheri clutched at the pillow, fury flashing in her eyes. "You can stop pretending to be my friend. I know whose side you're really on."

Alice sat back, stunned by Sheri's anger. She drew in a deep, careful breath. "I am your friend, Sheri. I'm on your side, and I care about you. I'm concerned for your future. I'll help you in any way I can, and if that includes a frank discussion—"

"Spare me the speech! I hear that you and Bradford-the-cold-heart talked all about it. I hear that you both think giving my baby away is a good idea."

Anger at Hayes barreled through her, stealing her breath. How dare he speak for her! How dare he use and twist her words for his own benefit! She harnessed her anger, resolving to deal with it—and him—later.

"Hayes and I did talk about the possibility of you and Jeff giving the baby up for adoption. I happen to think adoption is a wonderful alternative. But we talked in general terms. I would never pressure you to do something you didn't want to do. And I would never make plans *for* you. You should know me well enough to understand that."

Knowing that badgering the girl wouldn't get her anywhere, she stood. Sheri refused to meet her eyes, going so far as to turn her head away to avoid looking at Alice. "Let me tell you something else, whether you want to hear it or not. You can't emotionally blackmail Jeff into agreeing to marry you. That's not fair, and in the end it's going to hurt all three of you. It's going to hurt your relationship. Getting married, having and keeping this baby have to be right for both of you." She started for the door. "I suggest you think about it."

The teenager bent over the pillow for a moment, her shoulders shaking with the force of her feelings. After a moment, she looked up at Alice. "I don't care what you or anybody else says, I'm not going to give my baby away. I love it and I'm going to keep it no matter what."

Alice nodded. "If that's your decision, I'll support you in it. But I won't allow you to make that decision uninformed. I care about you too much."

Sheri began to cry again, great racking sobs of despair. Alice hesitated, then crossed to the door. As much as she longed to, now wasn't the time to try to talk to or reason with the girl. She was too upset. But Alice knew Sheri well enough to believe that when Sheri calmed down, she would consider what they'd talked about.

Alice stopped at the door. "If you need anything, just call."

The girl didn't respond, and Alice closed the door to the sound of Sheri's tears.

The evening passed, and Sheri didn't emerge from her room, although she accepted a dinner tray and made an attempt to eat. Alice hurt for the teenager and wished she could do something for her besides worry and pace.

She might have been able to help if Hayes hadn't planted in Sheri the seed of doubt about her motives. She paused in her pacing and frowned. Now the fragile bond of trust she'd formed with the teenager would have to be rebuilt. Until then, in the girl's eyes everything she said or did would be suspect.

Alice swore. She glared at the phone, willing Hayes to call so she could tell him off.

She whirled away from the phone and crossed to the window. Evening had long ago become night, and stars dotted the almost moonless sky. Had his visit the other night been about leveraging her? Had his kisses, his expression of need, been an attempt to buy her?

Ridiculous, she told herself, cheeks on fire. Hayes was a mature, intelligent man. Certainly he wouldn't resort to such a cheap, tasteless scheme.

But still... She caught her bottom lip between her teeth. He was desperate to find a way to separate Jeff and Sheri. He'd been trying for months before Sheri had even become pregnant. He was almost obsessed with the belief that Jeff's life would be ruined if he married now.

Would he go to such extreme lengths?

Alice turned and glared at the phone again, then strode to it. Without pausing for second thoughts she picked it up and dialed information, then Hayes's home number.

He answered on the second ring.

The sound of his deep, sleepy voice took her breath away. It reminded her of the long, hot afternoons they'd spent in bed, curtains drawn against the light, ceiling fan whirling, the cool breeze tickling their damp flesh. She muttered an oath and gripped the receiver so tightly her fingers went numb. "How dare you use me that way, Hayes?"

"Alice?"

"Yes, dammit, it's Alice. Don't give me any of your infernal lawyer double-talk."

He laughed. "I'm afraid you'll have to fill me in before I can say a thing. What are you talking about?"

"Your telling Jeff about our adoption discussion. Your intimating that we were plotting—"

"Plotting?" Hayes snorted in disbelief. "Where did you get that idea?"

"From Sheri. Who got it from Jeff." She curled her fingers around the phone cord. "So, Attorney Bradford, who do you suppose Jeff got it from?"

"Sheri and Jeff were talking about adoption?"

Alice heard the edge of excitement in his voice and gritted her teeth. He cared about nothing but getting his way. "Jeff brought it up. Sheri is hysterical."

Hayes let his breath out in a rush. "Do you know what this means, Alice? He listened to what I had to say. I can't believe it. He actually listened to me."

Fury took her breath. "And in your caution-be-damned rush to influence your son, you damaged my relationship with Sheri. Our discussion was nothing more than that. A discussion. I told you I wouldn't pressure her. How dare you use my words to try to influence—"

"Whoa! I mentioned to Jeff that we'd talked. That's all. I told him what your views were. Nothing more. Anything beyond that was either Jeff's or Sheri's interpretations."

"Why do I find this so hard to believe?"

"You tell me, Alice. You're the one making yourself out to be a victim."

Heat flew to her cheeks. "What do you expect me to think? You show up the other night, you're attentive, you're complimentary..."

Her throat closed over the words, choking them. She fought to clear it. "Is influencing Jeff what that was all about? If so, that was below even you, Hayes."

For a long moment Hayes said nothing. His silence echoed through her, taunting her. More than anything she wanted him to vehemently deny her accusation. The truth of that made her feel like a fool.

Hayes cleared his throat. "Wanting to make love with you has nothing to do with anything but wanting you. And that hasn't changed. I still want you. I still want to be with you."

She swallowed. Hard. "I see."

"Do you? Then see this, Alice. I think you want the same thing."

This time it was she who was silent. Her own silence taunted her as loudly as his had. Maybe louder. For as much as she wanted to deny the truth of his words, she couldn't.

"Alice? Nothing to say?"

She squeezed her eyes shut. "No," she whispered. "There is nothing to say. Except good night."

Hayes stared at the dead receiver for long moments before setting it back in its cradle, frustration building inside him. *Dammit.* He'd always been a man of action. Of purpose. It was one of the things that made him a good lawyer.

Yet lately, he'd been unable to find his footing, his sense of direction, of purpose. He vacillated between being positive he'd made the right decision twelve years ago to being certain he hadn't. One moment he told himself there was no place for Alice in his life, that she was better off without him; the next he was ready to chuck everything to be with her.

Tonight, if he'd been able to crawl through the phone lines, he would have. He'd wanted to touch her so badly he'd ached. He still did.

He stood and strode to the window. The moonless sky stared back at him, mocking him, his foolishness. He dragged a hand through his hair. Nearly forty and more unsure than at twenty, he thought, disgusted. His life more out of control. What a laugh.

He shook his head. How could she even consider that he had used physical intimacy as a way to drive a wedge between her and Sheri? Dear Lord, he had only to look at her to become aroused. He could think of nothing but touching her, making love with her.

"I need to talk to you."

At his son's quietly spoken words, Hayes turned. Jeff stood in his office doorway, ramrod straight, his expression determined. *His teenage son felt none of the uncertainties he did.* At least for now, father and son had traded places.

"Come in." Hayes indicated the chair across from his desk. "Have a seat."

"I don't think so. I'd rather stand."

In that moment, his son sounded like a man, not a boy. Hayes frowned. He crossed to the desk and faced his son. Wearily he took off his glasses and tossed them on top of the deposition he'd been reading before Alice's call. "Go ahead, Son. You've got my attention."

Jeff cocked his chin up. "The night of the storm, I went to the bridge. Where Mom died."

Hayes stared at his son, stunned silent. If Jeff had informed him that he'd grown a tail, he wouldn't have been more shocked. Jeff talked about his mother so seldomly that Hayes couldn't remember the last time. "I...don't know what to say."

The teenager cocked his chin another notch, as if preparing himself for a blow. "You think she killed herself, don't you?"

The words landed between them, flatly, baldly, their meaning altering the atmosphere around them. Hayes worked to keep his feelings from showing. "Where did you get that idea? The coroner ruled your mother's death an—"

"Accident. I know."

Jeff looked at the floor for a moment before meeting his eyes once more. In Jeff's eyes he saw a worldliness well beyond his eighteen years.

"I have ears, Dad. The family talks. The kids at school. When I was six I heard Aunt May whispering about it."

Hayes cursed May's big mouth. He cursed the human penchant for gossip. And he cursed himself for not being there for his son. "What do you want to know?"

"I want to know what you believe." Jeff fought visibly for control. "Tell me, Dad. The truth. Do you think Mom killed herself?"

Hayes swung away from his son and crossed to the window once more. The almost eerily dark landscape confronted him. Dear God, how did he answer that question? What could he say to his son to make everything all right? He touched his knuckles to the cool, hard glass. He couldn't make it all right—that was the problem. He was damned no matter what he said.

He swung back to face Jeff, swearing silently when he saw the flicker of hope in his son's eyes. It came down to principle. He'd never lied to Jeff. He wouldn't start now.

Hayes looked him straight in the eyes. "I have always suspected your mother meant to take her own life. Although I'll never know for sure."

Jeff flinched, his expression for one thin moment twisted with pain. Then he masked his feelings. Hayes ached for him. Ached to hold him, to assure him that it was all right to grieve. To hurt. To feel betrayed. But as much as he ached to do and say those things, he couldn't bring himself to act on the desire.

"Why?" Jeff asked, his voice thick. "Why'd she do it?"

"I don't know." Anger curled through Hayes, taking his breath. He tamped it down. "She was unhappy. Depressed. I couldn't reach her. I tried. I did."

"She didn't love me," Jeff said quietly.

Hayes could see that it took all of Jeff's strength to keep from crumbling. He admired his son, and he hurt for him. He had always hurt for him. He'd just never been able to show it. He'd always feared that if he did, his son would think himself weak, pitiable. He had feared his son wouldn't grow into a strong, confident man.

He took a step toward Jeff, hand out. "That's not true. She loved you very much. I remember the day she learned she was pregnant. She was walking on air she was so excited."

This time it was Jeff who spun away, who crossed to a window. Without turning, he muttered, "Don't sugarcoat it. I'm not a kid anymore."

"And I'm not sugarcoating it."

For a long moment Jeff remained silent. When he finally spoke, his voice vibrated with pain. "You know what the family says behind their hands? 'Poor little Jeff. His mother didn't want him.'"

Hayes swore. If even one of those gossips stood in front of him now, he would happily throttle him or her. "People talk," Hayes said fiercely. "That doesn't mean they know a damn thing. It only means they think they do. And that they like the sound of their own voices."

Jeff laughed, the sound choked and tight. "I remember her. Did you know that? My memories are so empty. And so hungry. I remember gazing at her and wanting...wanting so badly for her to touch me."

The teenager tipped his face to the ceiling, and Hayes saw how hard he worked to compose himself. When he met his father's eyes once more, his were suspiciously bright.

"If she'd loved either one of us, she couldn't have done it. But she did do it. Isn't that right, Dad?"

Hayes swallowed. Again he hadn't the faintest idea how to answer. Just as he hadn't the faintest idea what had prompted his wife. He searched for the right words, the ones that would comfort, that would heal. He prayed those words existed.

"It wasn't that she didn't love us," he began, groping. "But that she couldn't find peace with herself. That she couldn't love herself. Suicide is a selfish act, an act of total self-absorption. It didn't have anything to do with us, Jeff."

As he said the words, Hayes realized he believed them. After Isabel's death he'd gone to counseling. The words he'd just murmured to his son had been the counselor's, not his own. At the time of Isabel's death they'd rolled meaninglessly off him. But now...now he saw their validity. Now he understood.

Isabel's death had had nothing to do with him.

Something inside him shifted, then warmed. He drew a deep breath for the first time in what felt like forever. "You know what else? I may be wrong. Your mother's behavior was self-destructive, but that didn't mean that she meant to die. She didn't leave a note. She'd never threatened suicide. Maybe I tagged her behavior because I couldn't understand it."

"What's this?" Jeff snorted. "The indomitable Hayes Bradford wrong? That would be a first."

Hayes flinched, hurt by Jeff's anger, his sarcasm. "Have I been so arrogant?" he asked, moving around the desk, wishing he could reach his son, knowing in his gut that he was too late. "Have I been so...unmovable?"

"I'm going to marry Sheri."

Hayes stopped, nonplussed. "What?"

"All my life you taught me that a man stands by his actions. That a man does the right, the honorable thing. Now you want me to renege on those things you taught." Jeff shook his head. "Well, you taught me too well, Father. Because I won't. I got Sheri pregnant. I intend to marry her."

"But . . . Alice called tonight. She said that you and Sheri had fought, that you'd broached the subject of—"

"I did. It was a mistake." He clenched his hands. "I'm going to ask her to marry me."

"Don't do this, son. You'll regret it."

"The way you regretted your marriage?" Jeff laughed, the sound hollow, lost. "Sorry, my mind's made up. This is the right thing to do. I know it is."

"This is your life you're talking about. This will change it forever. Think about . . ." Desperate, Hayes searched for a way to convince his son he was making a mistake. A way to keep him from making it. "I'll let you off the hook. I forbid you to marry her."

"Same old story." Jeff narrowed his eyes. "You order—I obey. Sorry, that's not the way it works anymore. Besides, you don't get it. I'm not on a hook. I love Sheri. She loves me. She needs me. I want to marry her."

Hayes sucked in a sharp breath. "Marry her, fine. Despite what you think, I have nothing against the girl. Just don't do it now. You're too young. You have to finish your schooling. You have your whole life ahead of you."

"I can't learn while I'm married? I can still go to school, still get my degree and—"

"That's youth talking. Marriage and a family are a weighty responsibility. A consuming responsibility. Babies need food and diapers and shoes. They get sick, they have to go to the doctor. They need immunizations. How's Sheri going to take care of a baby and work? Or are you going to work full-time and go to school? And even if Sheri works, she's only seventeen. What kind of job is she going to get that will clear enough to pay for daycare and rent and food and everything else it takes to keep a family afloat?''

Jeff paled, even as he stiffened his spine. "I know I can do it. I'm going to marry her, no matter what you say."

Hayes sucked in a sharp breath. "Fine. Get married, but you're on your own. No Georgetown. I'm not paying. And I'm not going to support your family. You do this and you do it on your own. Totally."

"Blackmail? I can't believe you'd stoop so low. No, I amend that. I do believe it."

"If it's the only way I have to convince you, so be it."

Jeff took a step toward him, jaw clenched. "You've never wanted me to be happy. You've never wanted me to be loved!"

Hayes took an involuntary step back, stunned that his son could say such a thing, more shocked that he could say it with such conviction. "You're my son. I want you to be happy more than anything in the world." Jeff started to turn away; Hayes caught his arm. "Jeff, listen to me. I never—"

"I'm done listening." He shook off Hayes's hand and strode to the door. There he turned to face his father once more. "Just because you couldn't make your wife happy you think that I won't be able to make mine happy. Well, you're wrong. Dead wrong."

Chapter Seven

Hayes sat in his car, parked in front of Hope House, his son's words replaying in his head. *Just because you couldn't make your wife happy you think I won't be able to make mine happy.*

Hayes flexed his fingers on the steering wheel. Two days had come and gone, yet he'd been unable to put those words out of his mind. Just as he'd been unable to shake the way they had made him feel. Exposed and foolish. Again stunned that his son would say such a thing to him.

For a long time after Jeff had left him that night, he'd sat and stared at the empty doorway, reeling from Jeff's words, reeling with thoughts of Isabel and her death and, oddly, with thoughts of Alice.

Hayes gazed at Hope House, at the few lit windows scattered across its face. These days, things always seemed to come back to Alice. Their past. The way she made him feel. The ache that went away only when he was with her.

Hayes swore. When had his son become so perceptive? How long had he had the ability to look into his father's heart and soul and see what tormented him?

The hell of it was, Jeff had been right. He hadn't been able to make Isabel happy. Just as he hadn't been able to make his son happy, make him feel loved and cherished.

Yet he did love his son, did cherish him. So much, that at times he felt an almost desperate fear of losing him.

Hayes frowned. He was a cold man. A man who, for whatever reason, had an inability to express love.

He wanted to; he tried. And every time ended up mired in his own ineptitude. Lost. Helpless even. Hayes's frown deepened. *Helpless*. He hated that feeling more than any other. He hated the way it made him feel—like half a man. Like a man without the ability to control his destiny or take care of those who needed him most.

A shudder moved over him as he remembered the night Alice had lost their baby. As he remembered the way he'd felt—helpless to save their little one, helpless to take Alice's hurt away.

That night had been the worst night of his life.

He frowned again, fighting back the wave of frustration and pain that threatened to engulf him. How could he feel so deeply yet be so incapable of expressing those feelings?

He turned his gaze to Hope House once more. Alice's was the only car left in the lot. He imagined her in her office, oblivious to time, scrambling to save somebody. He smiled to himself. Alice had a bigger heart, a greater capacity for love, than anyone he'd ever known.

They'd been so ill-suited for each other it had been laughable. They still were.

Then why was he sitting here like a moonstruck teenager, his head swamped with thoughts of her?

Inside Hope House, a light went off. Twelve years ago, he hadn't made Alice happy. He hadn't been able to give her what she needed. He thought of her accusing words from the other night. *Why didn't you grieve? Why couldn't you comfort me?*

He looked at his hands. Big, strong hands. Capable of hard, physical labor, capable of breaking a man's nose with a single blow. Yet incapable of saving his child. Incapable of comforting the woman he'd loved. Incapable of real tenderness.

He pressed the heels of his hands to his eyes. What was wrong with him? Why hadn't he been able to comfort her? Lord knows, he'd wanted to.

He had felt as though he were dying inside. It had taken all his control to keep from falling apart, taken every scrap of fortitude he'd had to keep himself together so he could be strong for her. So he could be a man.

His throat closed and his chest tightened almost unbearably. He had loved their baby already. He had wanted it.

Another light popped off inside Hope House, then another and another, until the building stood almost eerily dark in the gathering night. Hayes waited, expecting Alice to emerge from the structure and walk to her car.

One minute became five, became ten. Hayes frowned, a trickle of unease moving through him.

Something wasn't right. Alice needed help. Even as he called himself an alarmist, he alighted from the car and strode up the walk to the porch and front door. He tried the door and found it unlocked.

His frown deepened. Foreboding replaced unease, and adrenaline began to flow through him. He shook his head. Alice was fine. The only problem here was his overactive imagination. Even as he silently intoned those assurances, he slipped inside Hope House, moving as quietly as possible through the dark interior.

He would find her safe in her office, he told himself, inching his way carefully toward the back of the building. He would find her chatting with a colleague and she would look at him as though he'd lost his mind. Considering their last discussion, she might order him to get the hell out.

For all he cared, she could throw a lamp at him. As long as she was safe.

Heart thundering, Hayes made his way through the cavernous old house, picking his way around furniture, careful not to make a sound. The place was obviously empty. It reeked of it.

Alice's office door stood ajar, light streamed from it, pouring into the hallway. Just as Hayes called himself a fool, he heard a sound. A guttural sound. A sound of fear. Alice's fear.

Something heavy hit the floor; Alice cried out; a male voice rasped an obscenity.

Hayes's blood ran cold. The adrenaline pumped through him so furiously it took every scrap of control, every bit of reason he had left to keep him from charging through her door. If he alerted whoever had

Alice to his presence, he would be no good to her at all.

He inched forward carefully. The floor creaked, and his heart stopped. He paused, waited a moment, then moved forward again. He reached the door and, holding his breath, ever so lightly eased it farther open.

Hayes caught his own sound of rage and fear a moment before it passed his lips. Alice was bent backward over her desk, a young man above her, a knife pressed to her throat. Her eyes, trained on her attacker, were wide with terror, her face bloodless with the same emotion.

Hayes swallowed, panic pounding frantically through him. The blade of the knife pressed into her soft white flesh, and he could see that just a fraction more pressure and it would cut her.

Dear God. Don't let him hurt her. Please... don't let him cut her.

Hayes eased the door open a fraction more and slipped into the office. Only then did Hayes notice the signs of struggle: the overturned chair and scattered books, the red welt on the side of Alice's face, the scratch marks down the boy's arm.

Luckily the boy was turned away from the door. Muttering and ranting, the teenager alternated between exerting pressure on the knife and easing off it.

The kid was high on something, Hayes realized, a sick feeling in the pit of his stomach. He could cut her without even realizing it.

Hayes took another step. Alice saw him. Her eyes flicked to his and her face went slack with relief. And for that one thin, bloodless moment, Hayes was certain the boy would see her expression and the direction of her eyes and become aware of him.

Alice must have feared the same thing, because she recovered quickly. "Don't do this, Tim," she whispered. "Please think—"

"Shut up," he hissed, fumbling with his belt buckle. "Say another word and I'll cut you. I promise I will."

Tears flooded her eyes as the blade pressed into her throat. A thin line of red marred her white skin. Hayes said a silent prayer and lunged. He grabbed the boy by his hair and yanked backward.

With a cry of surprise and pain, the boy fell against Hayes, knocking him into the wall. Hayes's head slammed against the old plaster, sending a spray of white from the ceiling, stunning him momentarily.

In that moment, Alice rolled off the desk and grabbed for the overturned phone; the boy kicked it out of her reach. Hayes lunged again. Whirling toward him, the boy slashed out with his knife. Alice screamed. Hayes stumbled backward, a hand to his chest, feeling the burn of the blade clear to his stomach.

Turning, the boy sprinted from the office. Even as Hayes told himself to chase after him, his legs buckled.

Sobbing, Alice ran to him. "Hayes…Hayes…" She knelt in front of him and grabbed his hands. "My God… are you all right?"

Hayes drew a deep breath, the oxygen clearing his head. He focused his gaze on Alice. "Did he hurt you? Did he cut you?"

She shook her head, tears slipping down her cheeks. "He didn't hurt me. But if you hadn't come…"

Hayes moved his hands almost frantically over her face and neck, assuring himself that she was, save for that one thin scratch, unhurt.

She shuddered. Hayes followed his hands with his lips, kissing her forehead and cheeks, her eyebrows, pressing his mouth to her eyelids, her nose, combing his fingers through her hair. "When I saw you... I thought... I was so afraid."

"Thank God you came." Alice clung to him. "Thank God..."

"If anything had happened to you..." He wound his fingers in her hair, unable to stop touching. Afraid that if he stopped, she would disappear. "I don't think I could have borne it."

"I'm fine... fine."

He drew her against him and for long moments held her tightly. Now that he saw she was safe, the ramifications of what could have happened hit him. It shook him to his core. "I could have lost you." He pressed his face into her hair, breathing in her sweet, unmistakable scent, letting it fill him. "Dear God, I could have—"

She cupped his face in her palms. "You didn't. I'm here."

With a groan, he caught her mouth and kissed her. Deeply. Ardently. And with more than an edge of desperation.

She returned his kiss in kind, moving her hands to his hair, twining her fingers in the crisp strands, anchoring him to her.

She trembled. So did he. He moved his hands everywhere, passionately, but more out of a gutwrenching need to be absolutely certain she was unhurt. That she was here, that she was with him.

He couldn't let her go. Not now. Not ever.

He dragged his mouth from hers, catching her ear, whispering words of endearment and fear. He found the pulse that beat wildly at the base of her soft throat; as he did he remembered the glint of steel there, the sliver of red, and held her tighter.

He could have lost her. Dear Lord, he could have lost her again.

He pulled a fraction away so he could look into her eyes. A dozen different emotions barreled through him, but he hadn't an idea how to express them. Tenderly he smoothed the hair away from her too-pale face, his chest aching almost unbearably.

"I'm fine," she murmured. "I am." She splayed her hands over his chest, over the thunder of his heart. His sweater was damp under her fingers. She lowered her eyes, then with a soft cry pulled her hands away.

Her palms came back red. Shocked, she returned her gaze to his. "You're hurt. My God, Hayes... he...cut you."

Hayes's face took on a stunned expression. He brought a hand to his chest as if feeling the wound for the first time since the blade had made contact.

She saw then that his sweater was soaked with blood, that the front of her blouse, from when they'd clung to one another, was also stained red.

She started to shake. Tim could have killed Hayes. He could have killed them both. With fingers that trembled so badly she could hardly control them, she explored the rip in his sweater, then the one in the shirt beneath. She drew in a deep breath, her stomach pitching. Tim's knife had had to tear through two layers of fabric to get to Hayes's skin. And had done so effortlessly.

Hayes touched his index finger to her chin, tipping it up. He forced a weak smile. "I'll be fine, Alice. I'm made of pretty tough stuff."

She tried to return his smile but failed miserably. Tears filled her eyes. "You're a lawyer," she told him softly, the words choked. "Not a policeman or soldier. Not a . . . a hoodlum."

He laid a gentle finger against her lips. "You haven't seen some of my court . . . battles—" He caught his breath and leaned his head back against the wall. He shut his eyes. "They can get . . . damn . . . bloody."

Her heart turned over. She knew how important it was for him to be strong. She could also see that the shock was beginning to wear off and he was beginning to hurt. She took a deep breath. "I'm going to take a look. Hold tight."

She eased the sweater over Hayes's head, saying a silent prayer of thanks for its heavy weave. Carefully she unbuttoned his shirt, then slipped it off his shoulders.

She winced at the sight of the wound that ran from the middle of his breastbone to the waistband of his jeans. It was red, raw and ugly. Sucking in a steadying breath, she probed it gently. He made a sound— just the smallest, swiftest intake of air, and her heart broke. She tipped her face up to his. "This is all my fault."

"No. You didn't—"

"Yes." She ever so gently kissed the wound. "My fault. I'm so sorry. So sorry."

He covered her fingers. His shook. "It's only a surface wound. Just enough to bleed like crazy and sting like hell."

"But it could have been—"

"It isn't."

She brought his hands to her mouth. Tears slipped from the corners of her eyes, spilling onto their joined hands. "How'd you get to be so big and brave?"

"Same way as every other guy."

"Your dad?"

"Yeah." One corner of his mouth lifted into a half smile, half grimace. "And Saturday-morning cartoons."

She shook her head, amazed that he could be so lighthearted now, when on a daily basis he was so serious and stiff. "Come, there's a first-aid kit in the bathroom." She helped him up and led him to the bathroom.

Hayes sat on the commode while she got out the bandages and antiseptic. She knelt in front of him, meeting his eyes. "This is going to hurt."

Again one corner of his mouth lifted. "I had a feeling you were going to say that."

Alice went to work. Luckily Hayes was right. It was only a surface wound and wouldn't require stitches. Heart pounding, she washed the gash, then, after soaking cotton with antiseptic, cleaned it.

He gritted his teeth. Her fingers shook. They didn't speak.

She finished cleaning, then went about bandaging the wound. She moved her fingers gently over his bare chest and abdomen, securing the tape.

When she'd secured the last piece, he covered her hands with one of his. She looked up; their gazes met and held. She didn't move; neither did he. Beneath their joined hands she felt the hammer of his heart, the firm warmth of his skin.

The smell of the antiseptic mingled with that of their fear. He trailed a finger across her eyebrow, down the curve of her cheek, over the softness of her mouth.

She gasped, the sound one of awareness. Of need. Her nipples hardened and pressed against her blood-stained blouse. At the apex of her thighs she grew warm, moist. She ached.

He lowered his head; she lifted hers more. Their mouths met. And clung. He dipped his tongue inside her mouth and stroked hers. She stroked back, the pulse beginning to pound in her head. Warm became moist; the ache became a throb.

He ended the kiss, drawing away from her as deliberately, as irrevocably, as he'd approached. And even though their mouths no longer touched, the effects of that kiss lingered.

Something had changed between them. She'd felt it in their kiss and in her heart; she saw it in his eyes. They'd changed with the kiss. With their brush with death. Some things had became so very important and some, now, mattered not at all.

"You've got to call the police," he murmured, his gaze still locked on hers.

"Yes. And Dennis." She started to stand; he stopped her. She searched his gaze. "What?"

He hesitated, then shook his head. "Nothing."

He released her hands, and they returned to her office. She shuddered as she stepped back into the room, seeing the physical evidence of the violence that had ensued. It could have been so much worse, she told herself. Tim could have killed Hayes. He could have killed her. Could have raped her. He'd intended to.

"Don't even think it," Hayes said, as if reading her thoughts. "It's over."

"I know. It's just that—" She shuddered again. "Will I ever be able to look at my desk and not...remember?"

He took her hands. "I haven't a clue. If you find a way to block it out of your mind, let me know. I don't think I'll ever be able to."

She gazed into his eyes for one long moment, then sighed. "I'll make those calls."

He released her hands, but never took his eyes off her, even while she used the telephone. He watched her intently. Possessively. The expression in his eyes almost fierce. She had the sense that he kept his gaze on her because he feared that if he looked away she would disappear. A shudder moved over her, one that was part fear, part arousal.

She hung up the phone and forced a weak smile. "You don't have to look at me like that. I'm fine. Really."

"I know." He cleared his throat. "That doesn't change anything. I can't stop picturing that bastard bent over you...the knife pressed to your—"

"Don't. Please don't." She curved her arms around herself and shifted her gaze. "The police are coming."

Hayes drew his eyebrows together. "I gathered."

"Dennis is going to call the rest of the faculty and warn them. Just in case..." She rubbed her arms, suddenly cold.

He held out his arms. "Come here, Alice."

She moved into his arms and clung. It felt like the most natural thing in the world. She buried her face into the crook of his neck, trembling.

He stroked her hair. "That boy—he's the one you told me about, isn't he? The one you had to kick out of the program?"

She nodded against his shoulder. "It was awful," she whispered. "I was working. Catching up on patient reports. Tim showed up. He was on something—I could tell. But I thought I could help him. That I could...talk to him. I thought he...needed me."

She drew in a ragged breath. "He was so angry. He said...awful, ugly things."

Hayes tipped her face up to his. "You don't have to do this, Alice. You don't have to tell—"

"Yes...I do. I need to talk about it." She squeezed her eyes shut, willing the nightmare images in her brain to disappear. "By the time I realized the situation...that Tim was out of control, it was too late. He had me trapped."

Hayes stiffened. "That son of a—" he swore, unable to contain his fury. "I should have gone after him. I could have caught him."

"And maybe gotten killed?" She shook her head. "No, Hayes. Never. Promise me."

Hayes did, and she relaxed against him. "He called me a two-faced...bitch. He said I was the cause of all his problems, that I was the reason he got kicked out of the program. He was so crazy, yet so...cold."

Hayes shuddered and tightened his arms around her. "He was the reason he got kicked out, Alice. Not you."

"I know, but—"

"No buts, Alice. The kid's a problem."

"I know. It's not that." She lifted her face to Hayes's. "It hurts because I did try to help him. It hurts that he could think those things about me. All I ever wanted was ... to help him." Tears welled in her eyes, then spilled over. "Please say you believe me, Hayes. I did try."

"I believe you." He stroked her hair. "You couldn't help but try. You were born to save people."

"Right. Tim came to me a troubled teenager with a drug problem. Now he's wanted by the police and will probably end up in jail. I did a great job, didn't I?"

"What's happened to him is not your fault. He was beyond your help."

She curved her fingers around Hayes's shoulders, sudden fear clutching at her. In the distance, she heard the wail of police sirens. "What if he comes back? What if he—"

"He won't." Hayes shook his head, his expression fierce. "I won't let anyone hurt you, Alice. Never again."

Chapter Eight

Jeff.

Sheri sat up in bed, and looked toward the dark window. Gravel sprayed against the glass once more, and she slid out of bed and padded to the window. After taking a quick peek behind her to make sure her bedroom door was shut, she eased the window up.

He stood below the window, the collar of his sweatshirt jacket hiked up around his chin, his face tipped up to hers. His nose was red from the cold, his hair tousled from the breeze. Her heart turned over. How could she stay mad at him when she loved him so much?

He thought they should give their baby away.

Their angry words of the other day raced into her head, and a tremor of fear moved up her spine. What if he meant to break up with her? After the way she'd acted, maybe he didn't love her anymore. If so, how would she go on?

She folded her arms across her chest. "What are you doing here?"

He shivered. "We need to talk."

She blinked against tears, the fear clawing at her. She clutched herself tighter. "You haven't called me in two days."

"You told me you never wanted to see me again."

"And you told me we should give our baby up for adoption."

He looked away, then back. "I'm sorry," he said. "I was wrong. Won't you forgive me?" When she didn't reply, he lowered his voice. "It's been hell without you."

Her eyes filled. "Then why didn't you call?"

"I had to do some thinking before I did."

"And now you've done that."

"Yes." He shivered again. "Can I come in?"

Sheri shook her head. "I promised Miss A."

"Then come out. It's really important." He looked up at her earnestly. "Please, Sheri. I—" He took a deep breath. "We need to talk about our future."

Our future. He hadn't come to say goodbye. Relief, sweet and breath stealing, moved over her. She nodded. "I'll come around."

Grabbing her robe from the end of the bed, she stepped into her slippers and checked the clock. Nearly eleven. She crossed her fingers and prayed Miss A. was asleep.

She tiptoed to the door and peered out. The lights she'd left on when she'd gone to bed were still burning, yet there wasn't a sign of Miss A. Sheri frowned. It didn't look as if she'd even gotten home yet.

That's right, Sheri remembered. Alice had said she would be working late. Catching up on something or other. Sheri doubled back to the bed and, using the pillows, created a shape that she hoped would pass for her asleep under the covers.

She bit her bottom lip, guilt plucking at her. She looked at the bedroom window and thought of Jeff waiting for her. "Our future," he'd said. Surely going out to talk with Jeff about something so important wasn't betraying Miss A.'s trust.

Squelching her misgivings, Sheri tiptoed out of the room and to the front door. She flipped out the porch light and stepped outside.

Jeff was waiting for her at the side of the porch, partially hidden by the row of oleander bushes. He took her into his arms. "I'm sorry, Sheri. So sorry. I didn't mean to hurt you."

She pressed against him. "I never should have said those cruel things to you. I didn't mean them."

"I love you so much."

"And I love you."

He kissed her, deeply yet sweetly. She pressed herself to him, holding on to him almost fiercely. The past few days had been the longest of her life, and even though nothing had been resolved between them, she knew everything would be all right. Somehow it would all work out.

Jeff ended the kiss, but didn't release her. He rested his forehead against hers. "I thought I was going to bust if I didn't kiss you soon."

She shuddered. "I know. I felt the same way. I've missed you so much."

"I never want us to be apart like that again," he said fiercely. "No matter what."

"Never," she repeated, shivering. "No matter what."

"You're cold. Come on, I parked the car around the corner."

He led her to the vehicle and opened the door for her. After she slid in, he went around to the other side. Once inside, he turned toward her, his expression serious.

She met his eyes, her heart beginning to thump uncomfortably against the wall of her chest. She drew in a deep breath. "You've been thinking about our future."

He set his mouth in a determined line, and a muscle worked in his jaw. "Yes."

She curled her fingers into the worn velour of her robe. Her chest ached so badly, she could hardly breathe. "What did you decide?"

"That we should get married."

Her heart dropped to her knees. She stared at him, certain she hadn't heard correctly.

He smiled and gathered her hands in his. "Yeah, that's what I said. Married. I think we should do it, Sheri."

She lowered her eyes to their joined hands, Miss A.'s warning running through her head. *You can't blackmail Jeff into marrying you. If you do you'll end up unhappy.* Sheri lifted her gaze back to his, tears blurring her vision.

Jeff's smile faded. "Don't you want to get married?"

"Oh, yes. More than anything. It's just that..." She caught her bottom lip between her teeth. "The last time we ... talked you seemed—"

"I needed some time to think. That's all. I love you." He put his hand hesitantly on her abdomen. She felt it tremble. "This is our baby. I think we should be a family."

"Oh, Jeff." Tears filled her eyes. "I'm so happy."

"So, you'll marry me?"

"Of course." Her tears brimmed, then spilled over. "How could you even think I wouldn't?"

He took her into his arms and cradled her against his chest. "I promise I'll be a good husband, Sheri. And a good father."

"I know you will be," she whispered, her voice thick. "And I promise to be a good wife. A good mother. Our baby is going to be the most loved baby ever."

He tightened his arms. "We're going to be so happy. We're not going to make any of the mistakes our parents did."

Again Alice's words came back to her. Were they already making a mistake? Had she blackmailed Jeff into marrying her? Would he live to regret this night? Would he grow to resent her? Their baby?

She tipped her head back to gaze up at him. His pensive expression took her aback. He didn't look sad, not exactly. But he didn't look happy, either.

A lump formed in her throat. More than almost anything in the world she wanted to marry him, for them to be a family. But only if he wanted to. She couldn't bear it if he was unhappy.

She touched her index finger to his chin. "Jeff?"

He met her eyes. "Yeah?"

"Are you...sure about this? Are you sure you...want to marry me?" He didn't respond, and her heart turned over. "If you don't want to, I'll still love you. What I said the other day, I didn't mea—"

He laid a finger gently across her lips. "I'm sure, sweetheart. I want us to be together. All of us."

"But..." She drew in a deep breath, torn between concern for him and fear that he really might back out. "What about Georgetown?" she asked, her voice shaking.

"It's out. Dad won't pay."

Her heart sank. "Couldn't you get a scholarship? You're really smart. Or...a loan, maybe?"

"Dad makes too much for me to get a loan. I already checked. And it's too late for a scholarship for next year. Besides, to be eligible for a scholarship I'd have to go to school full-time, and I'm going to need to work, too."

She caught his hand. "You have to go to school, Jeff. It wouldn't be right if you didn't. You've worked so hard."

"I figured I'd go to the University of New Orleans, or even Southeastern in Hammond. They're close and pretty cheap. I'll take a couple of classes and still be able to work full-time."

She remembered the day he'd gotten his acceptance from Georgetown, remembered how happy, how proud he'd been. Her heart hurt for him. "I can work, Jeff. I'll support us."

"You won't be able to after the baby comes. And even if we wanted to put him in daycare, I hear it's expensive."

She sagged against the seat back, fighting tears. "I didn't mean for this to happen," she whispered. "I didn't want to mess up your life."

"Hey." He turned her to face him. "How could you mess up my life? You're the best thing that's ever happened to me."

She pressed her face to his chest. She'd never been the best anything before. She loved him so much she would die without him. He loved her the same way. They were going to get married. Just as she'd prayed they would.

Then why did she have this awful feeling of doom, as if everything was going to tumble in on them?

She curled her fingers tightly into his soft fleece jacket, holding him to her. Beneath her cheek she felt the steady, comforting rhythm of his heart. She closed her eyes. They were going to be happy, the happiest couple ever.

And they were going to love their baby; it was going to be happy and healthy and beautiful. Their baby would never know the pain of abuse or neglect. It would never know what it was like to be unwanted and unloved.

"What do you hope it is?" Jeff asked softly, stroking her hair. "Boy or girl?"

She yawned. "I don't care. Either. How about you?"

"Either. A girl, maybe."

Sheri snuggled closer into his side, her lips curving up. They were going to be so happy people would look at them on the street and comment on it.

With that picture firmly in her mind, she drifted off to sleep.

The police's questioning brought all the horror back. Alice had answered their questions clearly and succinctly, even though exhaustion and the remnants of fear had pulled at her, sapping both her energy and peace of mind.

She'd clung to Hayes's hand, grateful for his support and unwavering strength. He'd stood protectively by her side, only speaking when directly spoken to, his expression grim. After the police had left, he'd insisted on driving her home. She despised being weak, but in truth doubted she would have been able to make the trip alone.

Alice glanced at him from the corner of her eye. What was he thinking? What was he feeling? Other than looking as if set in stone, his expression gave her no clue to either. She moved her gaze over him. He gripped the steering wheel with one hand; the other rested on his thigh. His mouth was drawn into a hard line and a muscle worked in his jaw.

He could have been killed tonight. She could have lost him.

She reached across the seat and laid a hand over his. He eyed her questioningly. What could she say? The truth? That she needed to touch him? To hold on to him? Hardly.

Instead she murmured her thanks.

"For what?"

"The ride, the support, coming to my rescue. For everything."

He replied by curving his fingers around hers. They drove the rest of the way like that, hands joined, neither speaking.

When they reached her house, Alice frowned at the dark porch. "I thought I left the light on."

Hayes stopped the car. He, too, frowned. "Sheri probably turned it off."

"Probably." She sounded unconvinced, even to her own ears.

"Wait here." He squeezed her fingers, then released them. "I'll take a look."

Fear turned the inside of her mouth to dust. She swallowed and shook her head. "No. I'll come. I'm sure you're right. Sheri probably turned the light off by accident."

They climbed out of the car and up to the porch. Without discussion, Hayes led and they both moved quietly, even stealthily.

Hayes tried the door. It was unlocked. He looked at Alice.

She started to shake. "Sheri," she whispered. "My God, what if—"

"Let's not jump to conclusions. She may have left it open."

"She's never . . . done . . ." Alice wrapped her arms around herself. "Maybe we should call the police."

"And say what? That your door's unlocked? I'll check it out."

She caught Hayes's hand. "He had a knife."

"I think we already established that fact," he said wryly.

As with a will of their own, her eyes lowered to his chest, to where the knife had made a path through the weave of his sweater. She lifted her gaze back to his. "Don't do this."

He laid his free hand against her cheek. "I'll be careful. I promise."

She tipped her face into his caress. She couldn't lose him. Not again. She didn't ponder what that thought meant or its ramifications; there would be plenty of time for that later. "Don't do anything heroic."

"Don't worry. I'm no hero."

He slipped into the house. Alice watched him disappear inside, a cry lodging in her throat. *No hero?* He very well may have saved her life tonight. He'd put himself in front of a knife for her. And now...

She swallowed the thought, the fear, and instead turned all her energy and attention to the dark interior of her house. Even though she strained, she heard nothing except the thudding of her own heart, saw nothing through the window but the shadowy outlines of her furniture.

Where was Hayes now?

Alice waited, her panic compounding by the second. Her heart beat so heavily against the wall of her chest she had to hold on to the porch railing for support.

Minutes passed. They seemed like hours. They should have synchronized their watches, she thought, a bubble of hysteria rising inside her. Isn't that what they were always doing in the movies? She and Hayes should have decided on a plan of action in the event he failed to emerge from the house in a designated amount of time.

She looked at her neighbors' on the left, then right. Both houses were dark. Still, if she pounded—

"Everything's fine."

Alice wheeled around, a hand to her throat. "Hayes! Thank God!" She launched herself into his arms.

He held her to him. "You're shaking like a leaf."

"I was so worried." She buried her face in the crook of his neck. "Anything could have happened."

She felt his smile. "Sheri is sound asleep. I checked under every bed, in every closet and behind every door. You and Sheri are perfectly safe."

Alice pressed her face into the warmth of his skin for one more moment, then drew regretfully away. "I guess that means I have to let you go."

"Not necessarily."

She searched his gaze, unsure what he meant. Unsure what she should do next. What she wanted to do next. She took a step back. "Thanks. Again."

"I'll walk you in."

"You don't . . . have to."

"But I want to."

She nodded and they walked inside. Her house looked exactly as she'd left it. Familiar and undisturbed. She breathed a sigh of relief.

"See."

She turned to Hayes. He stood beside her, real and solid. Unwavering in his support. Just as he'd stood beside her all night. Her breath caught. And she did see. Clearly. Maybe for the first time in weeks.

And she knew what she wanted. She wanted him to stay.

Her feelings had nothing to do with Tim or the ordeal she had been through tonight. They had nothing to do with the fact that Hayes had rescued her, or that he'd been hurt.

She ached for Hayes on an almost primal level.

Alice forced herself to draw a breath. It was crazy. Insane. This had been the worst night of her life, yet she was loath to let it go. Because she didn't want to let Hayes go.

But how did she ask him to stay?

Hayes cleared his throat. "If you're sure you're okay, I guess I should take off."

She caught his hand; hers trembled. Fear, different, sweeter and more potent than the fear earlier, pounded through her. "Hayes, I . . . there's—"

She couldn't find the words and dropped his hand. She spun away from him, curving her arms around herself. She called herself a coward and a fool.

"Alice?" He came up behind her and turned her to face him. Frowning, he searched her expression. "Are you sure you're all right?"

She wasn't all right. She doubted she would ever be all right again. She drew in a deep, ragged breath. *Ask him to stay. Ask him now.*

She took the coward's way instead. "Why did you . . . come to see me tonight? Why did you come to Hope House?"

He hesitated a moment, and she had the sense that he had to search his memory for the reason. A lot had happened since then.

"To apologize," he said finally, softly.

"Apologize? For what?"

"For discussing our adoption conversation with Jeff. I had no right. In my zeal to help him, I overstepped my bounds. But I didn't deliberately use you, Alice. I didn't mean to drive a wedge between you and Sheri." He lifted a hand to her cheek and stroked lightly. "And when I kissed you, there was nothing on my mind but making love with you."

Her heart tipped over. She took a deep breath. "Then don't go, Hayes. Stay. Make love with me."

He dropped his hand, obviously surprised. "Are you sure?"

"Yes." She lifted her chin. "I want you to stay with me, in my bed. My arms."

For a full ten seconds he said nothing. He didn't move, didn't seem to breathe. Those moments seemed like an eternity to her. Her chest tightened. What if he said . . . no? Dear Lord, what if he rejected her?

"I don't want to be a security blanket, Alice," he murmured, his voice low, thick. "I don't want to stay only because you're afraid of being alone."

She took a step toward him. "I want you to stay, Hayes. Not because I'm afraid of Tim or anything else. I want *you*. Tonight made me realize how much."

His eyes darkened. He lowered them to her mouth. "You're absolutely sure?"

She held out her hand. "Yes."

He stared at her hand for the space of a heartbeat, then grasped it. She curled her fingers around his. "Come."

She led him to her bedroom. It was dark. And cool. She shut the door softly behind them, then flipped the lock. Moonlight flooded through the windows, bathing the bed in a soft white glow, yet its light made the room's shadows appear deeper, darker by comparison.

He turned her toward him. As a blind man would, he moved his fingers over her face, tracing the line of her jaw, the arch of an eyebrow, the contour of her mouth. He'd been with her many times, but the way he touched her now told her that this time was special. The most special.

She followed his lead, touching, memorizing, drinking in the shape and texture that was Hayes. She remembered . . . everything. She wanted more than memories. Tonight she wanted reality, wanted the present instead of the past. She sighed. It had been so long, too long. Yet being with him like this felt familiar. It felt right.

And in a strange way, it felt as if they'd never been apart.

She trailed her fingers across his lips; he caught one with his teeth and pulled it inside his mouth. Her pulse scrambled; her knees turned to jelly. She sagged against him.

Hayes caught her mouth. Her head fell back, and he twined his fingers in her hair, the strands silky against his fingers. The pulse pounded in his head, a primal, heady beat. A beat that drowned out everything but his desire for her, a beat that refused to be denied.

She parted her lips; their tongues met and mated. She tasted fresh and rich and sweet. The taste of her went straight to his head, and he grew drunk on it. He dived deeper, yearning for more, for everything.

It seemed impossible that he held her in his arms this way; it seemed a cruel but delicious illusion. He'd thought he would never touch her like this again, had long ago faced the idea of life without the perfection of loving Alice.

The breath shuddered past his lips, and he moved his mouth to the silky curve of her shoulder, the gentle indentation of her collarbone. He'd never forgotten what it was like making love with her. He remembered the scent of her skin and the sounds of her passion; he knew where she liked to be touched, and which caresses would send her tumbling over the edge between arousal and ecstasy.

He should have refused her. She needed more than a man like him could give. She always had.

Even as frustration threatened to choke him, he acknowledged that he didn't have the strength of character to deny himself her. Not then. Not now. He wanted her with a ferocity that left him gasping.

He could have lost her tonight.

Hayes tightened his arms. He couldn't imagine a world without Alice. Hell, right now he couldn't imagine a minute without her, let alone the rest of his life. Yet soon he would not only have to imagine his life without her, he would have to face it.

Desperation clutched at him, and he muttered her name against her throat. Urgently. "It's been so long."

"Too long." She eased her hands down his back, claiming, possessing. "I've missed you. I've missed . . . this."

"You can't imagine how—" He trailed his mouth over her skin, nipping, tasting. "I've missed—" He nudged aside the collar of her blouse, sampling the sensitive, perfumed skin hidden there. "Being with you."

She arched her back as he found the swell of a breast. She curled her fingers into his hair. "Don't make me imagine any longer."

Hayes groaned, scooped her into his arms and carried her to the bed. He lowered her to her feet, into a pool of moonlight. The light welcomed, chasing away both the shadows and the uncertainties.

He never took his eyes from hers. "Are you sure, Alice? A moment from now will be too late."

"I've never been so certain of anything."

He smiled. Softly, and with infinite male pleasure. He made a move to take her into his arms; she laid a trembling hand against his chest, stopping him. "I don't want anything to mar this moment."

Slowly, deliberately, she stripped out of her violence-stained clothes. She tossed aside her blouse, her bra. Hayes followed her lead. He pulled his sweater over his head and tossed it aside. He unbuttoned his shirt and shrugged out of it. She slipped out of her slacks, he, his jeans.

As they undressed, Alice didn't take her eyes from his. Only when they had stripped away the last of their clothes did she allow herself the luxury of looking at him. Her breath caught. He was beautiful. Tall and lean and lightly muscled, with a scattering of dark hair.

And he wanted her. Just how much was extremely evident. She reached out and circled him with her fingers. He sucked in a swift, sharp breath; she smiled with pleasure.

The air was cool, Hayes's gaze hot. Her nipples pulled into tight, aching buds. Knowing what she wanted, he bent his head and drew one into his mouth, then the other. His lips feathered over her skin, raising chill bumps, arousing. She made a sound of pleasure deep in her throat and arched against him.

They came together, naked flesh to naked flesh. A ragged edge of his bandage scraped against her skin, a reminder of just how much she could have lost tonight. And just how precious life was.

Her pulse pounding in her head, she whispered his name over and over. *She wouldn't let him go. Not again. Not ever.*

He drew her onto the bed. She roamed his hard body with first her hands, then her mouth, delighting in his male textures, in the way he shuddered and moaned under her attention.

His skin grew hot under her hands, then slick. He eased her onto her back, pressing her into the soft mattress. His weight over her felt right. Nothing else had felt so right in a long time. Maybe ever.

She sighed as he claimed her, then pulled his mouth to hers. They moved together, slowly at first, then faster as their passion built to a blinding crescendo. Damp, gasping for breath, they soared to the heavens and beyond.

A cloud moved over the moon, stealing its soft illumination. Cloaked in darkness, she held on to Hayes. Their breathing evened; their skin cooled. The moon slid out from behind the cloud, and Alice bit back a sound of dismay. In those minutes of darkness Hayes's mood had changed. She saw it in the slight tightening in his features, in the regrets that raced into his dark eyes.

Emotion choked her. Reality had come too soon. The truth had reasserted itself rudely. He regretted their making love; nothing had changed or been resolved between them. He had hurt her before. He would again.

She had opened the door.

"I'm too heavy," he murmured. "I'll crush you."

He started to roll off her. She curved her legs around his, wanting to hold on to their perfect lovemaking for a few more moments. "You're not. Hold me a bit longer."

He did. He pushed the dampened tendrils of hair away from her face; he kissed her tenderly, he stroked her and murmured soft words of endearment. But she felt the way he distanced himself from her. Felt his second thoughts and second guessing.

She squeezed her eyes shut. How could she have been so stupid? How could she have forgotten the painful lessons of the past?

She opened her eyes and looked at him, her heart beginning to thud uncomfortably against the wall of her chest. She loved him. She'd never stopped. Dear Lord, how could she worry about making herself vulnerable to him, when he already owned her heart? Making love with him hadn't altered or heightened her feelings; she was as vulnerable to him as a woman could be to a man.

She drew in a deep, steadying breath. She had changed. She was no longer the naive girl who had worn her heart on her sleeve. She would not be crushed by a failed love affair. Nor would she stand anxiously by, dreading the moment when he would reject her.

"I don't expect anything from you, Hayes. No promises. No permanency. I'll make no emotional demands."

He drew his eyebrows together. "Where did that come from?"

Your eyes. You were looking trapped. She shook her head. "Considering our past, I thought we should get some things settled, right up front."

"Really?"

"Yes."

He rolled onto his side, bringing her with him. "Is there anything else you think we should settle?"

She thought for a moment, then shook her head again. "No. I guess that's it for now."

"Then it's my turn."

She met his gaze, steeling herself for whatever unpleasant announcement he was about to make. "Go ahead."

"You're incredible," he said seriously. "Spectacular. I want to make love again." He lowered his eyes to her mouth, then lifted them lazily back to hers. "And then again. You make me feel like a randy teenager, hot and bothered and one hundred percent horns."

She laughed, worries and regrets falling away from her. "Horns?"

"Oh, yeah." He eased the sheet downward, revealing her curves inch by inch. "Big ones."

"And that's what you want to get straight? Right up front?"

With his mouth, he followed the path of the bedding. "Well, everything else is already straight and—" he took her hand and guided it to him "—right up front."

"I see that." She laughed and curved her hand around him. "And what do you suggest we do about it?"

He made a sound of pleasure, deep in his throat. "Come here, gorgeous. And I'll show you."

Chapter Nine

Long after their hearts had slowed and their bodies had cooled for the second time, Hayes gazed at Alice. She lay beside him, eyes closed, her breathing deep and even, but he felt certain she wasn't asleep. Something about the way she held herself, about the tilt of her head, suggested instead that she was lost in her own thoughts.

Thoughts? Or regrets? He frowned. She'd surprised him with her announcement about not wanting or expecting anything from their relationship.

He moved his gaze over her. She'd changed so much in the years they'd been apart. The Alice he'd known had wanted a relationship almost desperately. She had longed for true love, total commitment and a storybook-perfect happily-ever-after.

His frown deepened. And yet she'd never married. Had never become a mother. Had he hurt her so badly? What an ego. She'd simply changed. Her priorities had shifted; she'd never found the right man.

As if sensing his scrutiny, Alice opened her eyes. The expression in them took his breath. In the space of that moment, she looked unbelievably sad. The moment passed and her expression cleared.

She lifted her lips in a lazy smile. "What's up, Doc?"

"At the moment, nothing."

"Too bad."

He trailed a feather he'd plucked from one of the pillows down the curve of her cheek. "I was thinking about you."

She colored with pleasure. "Good choice."

"Mmm." He bent and brushed his mouth across hers. "Very good."

She sighed. "Flattery will get you everywhere."

"A man can hope." He propped himself on an elbow and for long moments gazed down at her. A delicate pink flooded her cheeks, and she arched an eyebrow in question.

"I was wondering . . ." He shook his head. "Never mind."

"What?"

He sifted his fingers through her hair, shiny and dark against the white percale. "I was wondering why you haven't married. You wanted a family so badly I felt sure you would." She stiffened, just a bit, and he silently swore. "I shouldn't have asked. I'm sorry."

"It's not a big deal. It never seemed right, that's all."

He rubbed a few strands of her hair between his fingers. "I looked you up your senior year at LSU." She met his eyes, startled. "Through the folks at the coffeehouse. They told me you were engaged. I was happy for you."

"Were you?" She rolled away from him and sat up, pulling the sheet to her breasts. "Just think, if I had married Stephen you and I wouldn't be here right now."

Stephen. Hearing her former fiancé's name made the other man reel, and jealousy arced through Hayes. Had they been lovers? he wondered. Had they lain together like this, touching, whispering secrets and sharing their innermost thoughts?

The breath caught in his chest. Alice belonged to him. She always had. And even though she'd been engaged to that other man, rage at the thought of them together barreled through him.

Hayes regarded her profile, her expression, tight with hurt. Remorse replaced his jealousy of moments before. He caught her hand and brought it to his mouth. "I didn't mean to offend you, Alice. I knew how much marriage and a family meant to you. I was happy you were going to get what you wanted. That's all I ever wanted, you know. For you to be happy."

"Really?" She turned her face to his. "I find that hard to believe."

"It's true." He laced their fingers, unwilling to let her go. "I just knew I'd never be able to make you happy."

"Then why did you look me up, Hayes? What prompted that?"

He shifted his gaze. What could he tell her? The truth? That second thoughts and regrets had almost eaten him alive? That in a weak moment he had given in to them? Hardly.

He tipped his face up to hers. "I wanted to know how you were doing. I wanted to assure myself—"

"That I had survived your rejection?" She met his eyes, hers narrowed and angry. "Well, I did. And I was fine. Great, in fact."

"That's what I found out." He gazed at their joined hands a moment, then met her eyes once more. "What happened to him? This...Stephen?"

"I broke it off." She freed her hand. "It wasn't right. I didn't love him as much as I should have. He deserved better than that. He was a really nice guy."

She'd hurt the young man, Hayes realized. Badly. And it still bothered her. He understood her feelings only too well. He caught her hand once more, curving his fingers around hers. "I'm sorry."

"You needn't feel anything at all. It had nothing to do with you, Hayes."

Didn't it? Something in her eyes told him otherwise. Something in her eyes told him it had everything to do with him. He cursed himself for having hurt her. And he cursed his inability to love.

She drew her hand from his and brought her knees to her chest. She wrapped her arms around them. "What about you? Ever have the urge to remarry?"

"The closest I've come is with you."

For a long moment she didn't reply. Then she hugged herself tighter. When she spoke, she didn't look at him. "But that was different. That was because of the baby."

"Because of the baby," he repeated, frowning. "Yes. I'll never marry again."

She curled her fingers into the crisp white percale. "Just like that?"

"Just like that."

She took a deep breath, spots of color tinting her cheeks. "Trying to tell me something, Hayes?"

"Just the truth. I don't want to hurt you. I don't want to let you down."

"You're so arrogant. You're so sure you're the one who'll do the hurting." The color in her cheeks brightened. "I told you earlier that I don't expect anything from…this. But you felt you needed to warn me anyway. Well, you have, so why don't you leave?" She threw aside the sheet and started to climb off the bed. "In fact, we can just pretend this never happened."

He caught her hand. "I don't want to go. And I don't want to pretend this never happened, even if that were possible."

"No?" She inched her chin up, the coolly defiant gesture comical, given her flush of anger. "What do you want, Hayes?"

He gazed at her, his chest tight, his pulse fast. She was so beautiful, so special. She filled his life with warmth and light; she made him feel young and hopeful and completely without fear. She made him feel that maybe, just maybe, he could be the man she needed him to be.

Those things terrified him. Because he knew, in his heart and his gut, that he would never be that man. That he would never make her happy.

He couldn't bear to let her go.

He entwined their fingers and tugged her back to the mattress. "I want you. In my arms. My bed." He brought their joined hands to his chest, to his thundering heart. "From there, I'm not sure. I know I want you in my life. You make me feel good. Tonight, almost losing you made me see that."

Alice gazed at their joined hands, her own heart beating so heavily she had to struggle to draw an even breath. He didn't know what he wanted. He didn't know, not really, what their making love meant to him. If it had meant nothing, she could have dealt with that. If he knew, without a doubt, what he wanted—even if it wasn't her—she could deal with that.

But this...this gave her nothing to hold on to or give up on. How did she compartmentalize "You make me feel good" and "I want you in my life"? How could she temper her hopes and fantasies when he said things like that?

A part of her wanted to cry bitter tears of disappointment; another part wanted to sing with joy.

She lifted her eyes to his. "I think you'd better go. I need some time alone."

He hesitated, and for a moment she thought he was going to try to convince her to let him stay. Then he brought their joined hands to his mouth.

"Can I call you tomorrow?"

Her pulse fluttered, and she nodded. "Yes."

"If you have any...if you need anything, call me. Promise?"

She nodded again, touched by his concern, tears building behind her eyes. "I will."

They dressed quickly, and she walked him to the door. For long moments he gazed at her, then, without speaking, let himself out. She watched him cross the porch and descend the stairs, not moving from the window until he'd been swallowed by the night.

For a long time after, Alice wandered the house. She couldn't sleep, couldn't concentrate on a book; television didn't hold her interest. She tried drinking a cup of chamomile tea to settle herself down and, when that didn't work, a glass of wine. If it hadn't been so late she would have called Maggie for a soothing heart-to-heart.

Alice stopped at her bedroom door and gazed in at the rumpled bed. She'd tried to crawl back into it to sleep, but the sheets had smelled of Hayes. Of them, their lovemaking. She'd pictured them there, twined together, their hearts fast, their breaths short. And she'd remembered their last words to each other.

She swung away from the door. What did she want of him?

Everything.

The truth of that stole her breath away. She frowned and crossed to the front window. She wanted permanency. She wanted love and commitment. Happy-ever-after.

She hadn't even come close to being honest with him.

No, that wasn't quite right. She'd been somewhat truthful with him. She'd said she didn't expect those things from him or their relationship. And she didn't. She knew Hayes too well for that.

She squeezed her fingers into fists. This time, there would be no emotional complications. She wouldn't cling or cry. She wouldn't . . . need him so much.

This time, she vowed, she wouldn't give him a reason or an opportunity to reject her.

Pain and frustration pricking at her heart, she inched aside the lace drape and peered out at the dark porch and the even blacker road and river beyond. How had the situation become so hopelessly tangled so quickly? Knowing what she did about Hayes, how had she allowed herself to fall in love with him again?

She rested her head against the window frame, tears stinging her eyes. Had she ever stopped?

A figure separated itself from the shadows at the corner of the house. Alice's heart stopped, then started again with a vengeance. She brought her hand to her throat. *Tim. Dear God, Tim had found out where she lived.*

As she made a move to run to the phone, another figure emerged from the shadows, and the two embraced. It wasn't Tim outside her house, she realized. It was Sheri. And Jeff.

She drew her eyebrows together, confused. What was Sheri doing outside? Hayes had said the girl was fast asleep; he'd checked her room—

Turning, Alice raced to the guest room and opened the door. She crossed to the bed and realized instantly what Sheri had done.

Alice thought of how frightened she'd been when she'd come home and seen the dark porch, of how she'd panicked when she and Hayes had found the door unlocked.

She thought, too, of how much she trusted Sheri.

While she was being attacked, Sheri had been sneaking out to meet Jeff.

Sneaking. Her hands began to shake and she stuffed them into her robe's deep pockets. She'd thought she and Sheri were closer than that. She'd thought they had a better relationship than that, one based on trust and respect.

Anger and betrayal took her breath away, and she returned to the foyer to wait. Within moments she heard the key in the lock, saw the knob turn. Sheri stepped inside, glancing back once before shutting the door. Her lips were tipped up in a small, soft smile; her eyes were dreamy, satisfied. She looked like a woman who had just been with the man she loved.

Lost in her own thoughts, she didn't see Alice.

A ripple of envy moved through Alice. And longing, so sharp it stung. If only she could look—and feel—the way Sheri did right now: contented and happy, comfortable in the belief that she was loved.

Alice shoved her hands deeper into the robe's pockets. Instead she felt vulnerable, certain it was only a matter of time until Hayes rejected her again. Foolish for opening herself to that possibility, for not learning from the past's painful lessons. And ridiculously, irrationally, hopeful.

Sheri caught sight of her then and stopped in her tracks, the color draining from her face.

"Hello, Sheri."

"Miss A." The words came out as a dismayed squeak, and she cleared her throat. "What are you doing...up?"

"That's an excellent question." Alice took a step toward her, working to control her anger and hurt. "What were you doing up...and out?" She moved her gaze pointedly over her, taking in the nightgown, robe and slippers.

Sheri swallowed. "It's not what you think."

"No?"

She shook her head. "Nothing happened. Jeff came by and...he needed to...talk."

"Why didn't you ask him in?"

"It was late and...I..."

"It was too late to have him in, so you went out?" Alice folded her arms across her chest.

"Yes." Sheri hung her head. "But we weren't doing anything. We just talked. I fell asleep."

"Sheri, it wouldn't matter if you'd snuck out to go to church. It would still have been a lie. It would still have been wrong. Can you explain your reasoning to me?"

Sheri shook her head, not lifting her gaze. "Are you mad?"

"Yes. And hurt." Sheri glanced up at her then, obviously surprised. "You betrayed my trust. By sneaking out. With the thing you did with the pillows to try to trick me. That hurts, Sheri. I thought we had a better, more honest, relationship than that. If it was that important to talk to Jeff, you should have asked him in. I would have understood."

Alice could tell by Sheri's expression that she didn't quite believe her. She took another step toward the girl. "I'm not like your parents. I'll treat you with respect if you treat me the same way. I want to trust you, Sheri. I really do."

The teenager's eyes filled with tears. She wrung her hands and battled to keep them from spilling over. "You're going to kick me out."

Alice's heart turned over. Sheri expected complete rejection at every turn. "Just because I'm angry doesn't mean I'm going to abandon you. Or stop caring about you. You're still a minor. I'm responsible for your safety and well-being. Anything could have happened." The image of Tim with the knife filled her head, and she shuddered. "Do you understand?"

"Yes... it's just that..." She shook her head. "I understand."

"What is it, Sheri? Don't hold back."

"It's just that, when my parents, you know, got angry, they..." Sheri looked helplessly at Alice, her eyes brimming with tears.

Alice's chest tightened. Sheri's parents became enraged for no reason at all; their anger would turn to violence, and would continue to simmer even after the violent act. No wonder Sheri feared the emotion.

"It's okay to be angry. It's a human emotion. It happens and has to be let out. It's only a problem when it comes out sideways. Or when it has nothing to do with the person it's directed at. Or when the person can't stop being angry. I was angry because you deceived me." She touched Sheri's hair lightly. "We've talked about it. Now it's over."

"Miss A., I'm ... sorry I tricked you. I won't do it again. You mean ... so much to—" The girl drew a shuddering breath. "I wouldn't want to hurt you for anything."

Alice hugged her, tears stinging her eyes. "You mean a lot to me, too." She drew away so she could see Sheri's expression. "I take it everything's okay between you and Jeff?"

Joy lit Sheri's eyes. "We're going to get married. That's why he came over. To apologize for the other day and to ask me, you know, to marry him."

Alice thought of Hayes, of how disappointed he would be. "Does his father know?"

Sheri's smile faded. "I think so. He told Jeff he wouldn't pay for college if we got married. That means no Georgetown."

"I see."

"Don't look like that." Sheri shook her head, distressed. "He'll go to UNO or Southeastern. He's got it all planned."

"Does he?" Alice drew her eyebrows together in thought. "But how does he feel about it? You're sure it's what he wants?"

"Yes." Sheri stiffened and took a step away. "I didn't blackmail him into marrying me, if that's what you mean. It was his idea, and he wants to. I asked— to be sure."

But a decision like this was so much more compli-cated than that. Alice knew from experience. "I didn't say you blackmailed him, Sheri."

"The other day you did." She inched her chin up defensively. "And it's not true."

Alice's heart went out to her, but she couldn't drop the matter just yet. "I just wanted you to think long and hard about what you wanted. The decision you're making will affect the rest of your life. I want you to be happy. That's all."

"We will be," Sheri said fiercely. "We already talked about it. We decided on it."

Alice forced a smile, unable to fully shake her feel-ing of unease. "I'm glad for you both."

Sheri lowered her gaze, her lips curving with plea-sure. "Thanks. Miss A.?" She lifted her gaze almost shyly. "Would you . . . be my bridesmaid? We proba-bly won't, you know, have a real wedding, but even if we go to the courthouse I'll need someone to stand up for me. I'd really like it to be you."

"I'd love to."

Sheri beamed. "Really?"

"Yes, really. Goose." Alice hugged the teenager again. "Now, I think it's time we both went to bed. Tomorrow's work and school."

Sheri nodded and yawned, as if the very mention of sleep had brought on fatigue. "You're the best, Miss A. Good night."

"Good night," Alice repeated, watching the teen-ager walk to her room. When the girl had closed the door behind her, Alice's thoughts returned to Hayes. Did he know about Jeff and Sheri's plans? Surely he'd discovered Jeff missing when he'd gotten home tonight. Knowing Hayes, he was dealing with his son at this very moment.

She looked at the phone, indecision pulling at her. Should she call him?

She would wait, she decided, flipping off the light. He'd said he would call her tomorrow. That would be soon enough to discuss Sheri and Jeff's engagement with him.

Hayes didn't call. Morning became afternoon, afternoon evening. Alice glared at the phone for about the billionth time since arriving home from work.

Her day had been a nightmare. She'd talked to the police twice. Tim hadn't been picked up until nearly five. The Hope House faculty had met to discuss the incident, and a student with an uncle on the police force had heard the story and it had spread through the students like wildfire. She'd spent a good part of her day meeting with students, assuring them that she was fine and that they had nothing to fear.

All in all, she'd spent eight hours reliving the incident, every terrifying moment, over and over again.

When she'd gotten home, she'd found Sheri pale and shaken, waiting for her. Sheri, too, had heard about Tim and was extremely upset. During their discussion about the incident Sheri had started feeling nauseated and then went to lie down in her room. Alice had phoned the doctor for advice.

Sheri had confessed that she'd been nauseated a lot, but that she hadn't wanted to tell Dr. Bennett for fear the woman would find something wrong. That confession had prompted another discussion, one about Sheri's health and the baby's, and the importance of absolute honesty with her doctor.

Alice looked at the phone again. Hayes had said to call if she needed anything. But she hadn't called, even though she had needed him badly. Had needed to hold on to him. Had needed his strength. His comfort and support.

She'd needed to know he was there for her.

Frustrated, she swung away from the phone. She'd be damned if she would let him know how much she needed him. How much his silence today had hurt. And if she called him, he would know. He would hear it in her voice.

A knock sound on the door, and she jumped. *Tim.* She stared at the door, gooseflesh racing up her arms, fear closing around her throat like a killer's hands.

Tim had been picked up hours ago, she reminded herself. Even though she knew he couldn't hurt her, she moved hesitantly toward the door. The knock sounded again, this time louder, more insistent. Drawing in a deep, steadying breath, she peeked out the sidelight.

Hayes stood on her front porch, his arms loaded with flowers and bags of takeout.

And he looked exhausted. His hair was tousled either by the wind or his own fingers; he'd removed his jacket and loosened his tie; worry and fatigue were etched around his eyes and mouth.

Her heart turned over, and she unlocked the door and swung it open.

He smiled and moved his gaze slowly over her. "Hey."

His gaze turned her knees to pudding, and she held tightly to the door frame for support. "Hey."

"Have you eaten?"

She shook her head, feeling hungry for the first time all day. "Only an apple. Earlier."

He indicated his loaded arms. "Shrimp po'boys."

She smiled. "My favorite."

"And roses. But those aren't to eat."

She pouted. "Darn. And I had my heart set on them."

His lips curved. "Well, in that case, I'll eat the sandwiches and you can have the flowers."

"You're all heart." She swung the door wider and stepped aside so he could enter.

He looked around. "I brought an extra po'boy for Sheri. Is she here?"

"Asleep. She's not feeling well." Alice took the flowers and held the bouquet to her nose, willing her heart to stop fluttering. She felt like a silly, breathless teenager. "They smell divine."

"I thought you could use them. Today must have been rough."

She swallowed the words that rushed to her lips, the ones about her fears and exhaustion and concern. The ones that would tell him how she'd longed to hear his voice. How she'd waited for his call.

She wouldn't be needy. She wouldn't cling.

She forced a casual smile. "I'm fine. Come in. I'll put the flowers in water."

He followed her to the kitchen and set the take-out bags on the counter.

"Would you like a beer? There's some in the fridge."

"Thanks." He took one from the refrigerator and popped the top. "What a day."

She angled him a glance. "Bad?"

"Ridiculously so."

He tipped his head back and drank, and Alice gazed at the arch of his throat, then lowered her eyes to his open collar. She imagined her lips there, imagined the taste, the texture of his skin. She dragged her eyes away, uncomfortably aroused by the simple act.

And by the situation. They had acted out this scenario time and again nine years ago, spent an hour in the evening, after Jeff had gone to bed, talking about their day. He'd talked about the trials and tribulations of being a lawyer, she had amused him with stories from the coffeehouse. She had looked forward to those times.

"I have a client who I suspect is insane."

She laughed softly and put the roses in the vase, fiddling with them. "That sounds like a bit of an overstatement."

"You tell me. You're the shrink."

"'Counselor.'"

He smiled. "Okay. Counselor. He rants and raves. He wants me to do things that are borderline illegal and definitely unethical. Although he can't give me any specifics, he's certain everybody is out to ruin him, and today he informed me that he has mob connections, and if I can't get things done above the law, he'd seek other methods. What's your professional opinion?"

"He doesn't sound like somebody with a firm grip on reality. And he doesn't sound pleasant to work with." She carried the flowers to the table, set them in the center, then began gathering the utensils they would need for dinner. "What are you going to do?"

"The firm wanted to take care of him because he's the brother of one of our most important clients. But the senior partners met late this afternoon, and we've decided to suggest he find other representation."

She took the plates out of the cupboard. "I had no idea corporate law was so exciting."

Hayes laughed and crossed to stand behind her. "Usually it's deadly dull." He sifted his fingers through her hair. "But I don't want to talk about work."

Her hands stilled; her pulse scrambled. "No?"

"No." He buried his face in her hair. "God, you smell good. Like wildflowers and honey." He made a sound of pleasure. And pain. "I couldn't stop thinking about you today. About us."

She breathed deeply through her nose. *Keep it in perspective, Dougherty. This means nothing.*

He turned her to face him. "The day was hell. I sat with the partners and imagined you naked, my hands on you. I listened to my crazy client rant and imagined my mouth on yours, our tongues twined. I thought about making love." He drew her against him, whispering his mouth over her face, her neck. "Did you think about me? Even once?"

Try a million times, Hayes. Alice lifted her face to his, her heart beating fast, her skin growing almost unbearably warm. "Once. Or twice."

He laughed softly, the sound thick with arousal. He trailed his fingers across her collarbone, then lower, over her breasts. Their peaks stood at attention, pressing against the light weave of her sweater, begging for another caress.

He answered their plea with his palms, brushing softly across them. Her head fell back; her lips parted. He brought his mouth to hers, stopping when it hovered a fraction above. "Did you think about making love? Did you think about this?" He moved his hands lower still, and she gave a small, strangled moan of pleasure and arched against him.

"No," she murmured, trembling. "Not once."

"Liar." He laughed and pressed her back against the counter. "You should be ashamed."

She should be. Ashamed that she wanted him so badly. Ashamed that she would throw away everything she knew to be smart and safe, just to be with him. Her heart. Her well-being. Her reputation.

Sheri. Alice laid her hands against Hayes's chest. The girl slept in the other room, only a matter of feet away. The hour was early; she could still awaken. And come out to find her and Hayes in a passionate clinch.

Alice flattened her hands and pressed. "Hayes... this isn't a good idea. Not now." She drew in a deep, shaky breath. "Sheri's here. She could...wake up and...and find us."

He groaned and rested his forehead against hers. Beneath her hand she felt the wild beat of his heart, felt his muscles, tight with strain.

"Are you all right?" she asked softly.

"Hell, no." He growled in her ear. "I'm in a major amount of pain."

She laughed, the sound feminine and pleased. "A major amount?"

He captured her hand and brought it to him. "Major."

She didn't move her hand. "Maybe food will help."

"Lady...there's only one thing that's going to help."

He rotated his hips, and she snatched her hand away. "Oh, no, you don't."

He caught her and dragged her back to his chest. "What if I told you I'm going to die if I don't have you."

She saw the twinkle of amusement in his eyes and played along. She arched an eyebrow. "I'd tell you that's a very old and tired line."

"Yeah, but this time it's true." He pulled her a fraction closer.

"What about it, Dr. Dougherty? Prepared to make a promise you have no intention of keeping?"

She stood on tiptoe and whispered in his ear, outlining exactly what she would do—later. She pressed her mouth to his. "And that's a promise I look forward to keeping."

Chapter Ten

The po'boy sandwiches were delicious. On crusty French bread, they were thick with fried shrimp and sloppy with mayonnaise, tomato and lettuce. She and Hayes ate in silence, using the food as a way to ignore the awareness crackling between them.

And as they did, both watched the clock, counting the minutes, silently urging the seconds to tick by at an accelerated pace.

Instead time seemed to crawl.

Alice took a bite of her sandwich, which tasted at once delicious and like cardboard. She found herself gazing at Hayes, watching him eat, her eyes fastened hungrily on his mouth.

And she found him gazing at her the same way, with the same longing, the same hunger.

She pushed away the last of her sandwich and shifted in her seat, arousal clawing at her. "This is agony."

He, too, pushed away his sandwich. He glanced at the clock. "I'm dying here, Alice."

"Me, too." Alice thought of the way she'd pressed her hand against him, and a shudder moved over her. She wanted to do it again. Now. She felt like some sort of wanton woman, some sort of hussy.

She flushed and looked at her hands. "Please, let's talk about something, anything but . . . you know."

A smile tugged at the corners of his mouth. "Yeah, I know. Boy, do I know."

Silence stretched between them again. They both glanced at the clock. Hayes cleared his throat. "When's late enough? Ten?"

She swallowed. "Maybe."

"It's nearly that now."

"It's nine-twenty."

"Like I said, it's nearly ten."

She took a deep breath, feeling as if she were grasping at straws. "How was Jeff this morning?"

Hayes shook his head. "I don't know. He spent the night at his cousin's in Metairie."

"At his cousin's?" she repeated, frowning.

"They had an out-of-town ball game today, and instead of driving across the causeway in the morning—"

"So you didn't talk to him last night, either?"

"No." Hayes frowned. "What's going on?"

Dammit. Alice caught her bottom lip between her teeth. She should have called. "Hayes, we need to talk."

His frown deepened. "Why do I have the feeling I'm not going to like this?"

She wished she could assure him otherwise; instead she jumped right in. "Last night Sheri wasn't in bed when you searched the house for Tim. The door was unlocked because she'd snuck out to meet Jeff and forgotten to relock it."

Hayes straightened. "Jeff was here?"

"They were parked outside. Around the corner."

Hayes swore and stood. He crossed to the window above the sink and for long moments stared out at the dark night. "He lied to me," he said softly, not turning. "I got home and found a message on the machine. He told me he was staying with Stan. Because of the game." He laughed, the sound hard and laced with self-derision. "I didn't check up on him. I didn't doubt for a second that he was telling me the truth."

"I'm sorry."

He swung around to face her. "Why didn't you call me?"

"I thought about it." She spread her hands. "It was late, and by the time Sheri and I had talked, I figured he was home. Already doing battle with you."

Hayes swore again. "This situation is getting out of control. I'm worried about him. I'm worried about his grades. In these last months of school he could blow his entire senior year."

"There's more." He met her eyes; in his she saw trepidation and resignation. "Jeff asked Sheri to marry him. She accepted."

"Damn." Hayes pulled a hand through his hair. "Jeff told me he was going to, but I'd hoped . . ."

The look on Hayes's face was so bleak Alice had to work to hold back a sound of pain. She stood, crossed to him and cupped his face in her hands. Beneath her palms, his cheeks were rough with the beginnings of a beard. "They love each other so much, Hayes. They want to be together. They have that on their sides. And she's a good girl. A really good person."

"He's making a mistake," Hayes said tightly, battling, Alice saw, for control. He covered her hands and looked deeply into her eyes. "They both are. Why can't they see that?"

"Think of this as a beginning, Hayes. Not an end."

"I wish I could." He dropped his hands and stepped away from her, turning again to face the black night. After a moment, he looked over his shoulder, meeting her eyes once more. "It's not Sheri. Believe me, Alice, I have nothing against the girl. It's everything else. I wish there was something I could do, some way I could get Jeff to see reason."

Alice thought of Maggie and Royce, of their devotion to each other, and tears sprang to her eyes. She caught Hayes's hand. "They're going to do this, Hayes. Help them. Try to understand."

"I don't know if I can." He curved his fingers around hers. "I'm no good at things like this. At being empathic. Or understanding. For me, there are only good choices and poor choices. Will you help me?"

"If you really want me to."

"I do." He pulled her toward him. "I really do."

She ran the flat of her hands up his chest, curving them around his shoulders. She moistened her lips. "I wish I hadn't brought up Jeff and Sheri. It's spoiled the mood."

He lowered his mouth to hers, stopping when it hovered only a breath away. "It hasn't spoiled mine."

She pressed herself against him, her pulse fluttering at his obvious arousal. "No?"

He nipped at her lower lip, mock-growling. "What time is it?"

She smiled against his mouth. "Late enough."

"Thank . . . God." He captured her mouth, kissing her in a fever of need and too long denied desire. She returned his kiss in kind, clinging to him, telling him without words how much she desired him, how much she'd missed him.

With a muffled groan, Hayes swung her into his arms and carried her to her bedroom.

The bed waited, big and soft and yielding. They sank to the mattress, lips still pressed together, neither willing to part for a moment, even to make themselves more comfortable.

Their lovemaking was at once desperate and tender, passionate and languorous. Hayes took a long time loving her, arousing her to a fevered pitch with his hands and mouth, taking long moments to sample soft, perfumed places, ones that begged for his caresses and, after having received them, throbbed in thanks.

Alice arched and sighed, twining her fingers in his hair as he brought her to the brink but not beyond, over and over again. When he finally joined with her, she cried out his name and clutched him to her. She hadn't a doubt that if she died and went to heaven, heaven would be eternity in Hayes's arms.

Hayes held on to her just as tightly, and although he murmured words of passion, not love, she sensed a need in him, an urgency that had nothing to do with passion, a need she'd never sensed in him before.

He needed her. Tears stung her eyes, and she blinked against them, horrified that he might see. She'd never really felt that he'd needed her before. Twelve years ago he'd ended their relationship and had seemed to go on without pause.

Hope, sweet and sanity stealing, blossomed inside her. Maybe, just maybe, she and Hayes could have that happily-ever-after after all.

She smiled and pressed a kiss to his damp chest. "That was wonderful."

He tangled his fingers in her hair and tilted her face up to his. "You were wonderful."

"Was I?"

He kissed her long and hard. "Yes."

She searched his gaze. "When do you have to go?"

"Soon. I wish I didn't have to, but Jeff is due home soon." Hayes's expression darkened. "At least according to the information he gave me last night. I found out just how trustworthy that information was."

She laid a finger against his lips. "Don't. Not now."

"I'm sorry." Hayes brushed the dampened tendrils of hair away from her face. "Lord, you're beautiful."

She flushed with pleasure and snuggled against his chest. "Five more minutes, okay?"

"Not nearly enough."

"But more than nothing."

They fell silent. The clock ticked out the five minutes. Just as Alice opened her mouth to ask for five more, the phone rang. They looked at each other, then laughed.

Alice sat up and pulled the blanket to her chin. She checked the clock, noted it was nearly eleven and reached for the phone, picking it up on the third ring. "Hello," she murmured, her voice still thick with passion.

"Alice . . . baby, is that you?"

Alice's blood went cold. She recognized the gravelly voice, recognized the slight, alcohol-induced slur. From her past. And her nightmares.

She glanced at Hayes from the corner of her eye. He had climbed out of bed and begun dressing. Why now? she wondered, feeling helpless and trapped. Why had her mother chosen this moment to call, when she was feeling so happy and hopeful, why when Hayes was present and able to overhear and deduce what was going on?

Alice cleared her throat. "Yes, this is Alice Dougherty."

"Baby, it's me. Your mama. Don't you recognize my voice?"

Alice started to tremble; she squeezed her eyes shut. How could her mother even ask? The sound of her voice played over her senses, calling so strongly she could almost smell the sickly sweet odor of bourbon, feel the sticky wet of sweat on the back of her neck, the burn of fear in the pit of her stomach. And hear the sound of flesh smacking flesh.

You lazy brat . . . you'll never amount to nothin', you hear me? You'll never be more than a lazy, good fer nothin' little mouse.

Alice curled her fingers tightly around the phone cord. "It's been years."

"Too long for a mother and daughter to be apart." Her mother paused, as if waiting for a comment from Alice. When none came, she went on. "You haven't answered my letters."

"No." The word came out as a strangled whisper, and Alice cursed it. She wanted to be strong and forthright and confident. Not the frightened little mouse she was now.

"I want to see you."

Hayes stopped dressing and looked at her. Alice met his eyes, then glanced quickly away. She didn't want him to know about her mother's reemergence in her life. She didn't want to talk about it with him; if she did, she wouldn't be able to stop herself from falling apart.

No emotional complications, she told herself. She couldn't be too needy. She couldn't cling.

"Alice?" her mother repeated. "I want to see you."

Say no. Tell her you're not interested. Alice tightened her fingers on the phone cord. "This really isn't a good time. You'll have to call back another. Goodbye."

She hung up the phone, her heart beating so heavily she could hardly breathe. Disappointment spiraled through her. What had happened to the confident and independent woman she recognized herself to be? She hadn't even had the guts to tell her mother the truth.

Maybe Hayes had been right about her all those years ago. Maybe she hadn't changed as much as she thought. Tears stung the back of her eyes. Maybe she was a fool to think things would work out between them this time around.

"Alice? Is something wrong?"

Alice met Hayes's gaze, fighting to keep her distress and uncertainty from showing. She wouldn't allow him to think she was the girl he'd known all those years ago, even if she'd started to believe she was.

She forced a cocky smile, threw aside the sheet and climbed out of bed. "Not at all. Why do you ask?"

"That call." He drew his eyebrows together. "You sounded strange."

"Did I?" She slipped into her robe, her hands trembling so badly she could hardly tie the belt. "I'm tired, that's all."

He tucked his shirt into his slacks. "Who was it?"

"No one."

Hayes's hands stilled and he studied her, frowning. "Really? No one?"

Who could blame him for not believing her? "No one" didn't call at eleven p.m. "No one" didn't make her react so strangely. "It was an acquaintance from my past. Someone I didn't part on good terms with. That's all."

He searched her expression, and it took all her strength to keep from crumbling. "Was it...Stephen?"

"Stephen? My old fiancé?" She shook her head, a smile tugging at her mouth, chasing away some of the unpleasantness of her mother's call. "No. It wasn't even a man. But thanks for thinking so."

He crossed to her and took her into his arms. "The thought of you even talking to another man makes me crazy with jealousy. The thought of you doing it from your bed at eleven p.m. makes me want to grab you by the hair and drag you off to my cave."

"Mmm." She rubbed against him. "I like bringing out the barbarian in you."

"Save that thought." He pressed his mouth to hers, then drew regretfully away. "I've got to go. Are you okay?"

"I'm fine." She resisted the urge to sag against him and smiled brightly instead. "I'll walk you to the door."

When they reached it, Hayes kissed her, long and hard. Then, with a whispered good-night, he left. Alice watched him from the doorway, her chest tight and aching. A moment before the dark swallowed him, he stopped and looked over his shoulder at her, his expression quizzical. She blew him a kiss, then drew back into the house and closed the door.

Trembling with a combination of fatigue and hopelessness, she rested her forehead against the door. From outside she heard a motor roar to life, then tires crunch on gravel as Hayes pulled away from the curb.

Gone. Hayes was gone. Alice drew in a deep breath. But only for now, for tonight. She would see him tomorrow or the day after.

But which time would be the one when he left her for good?

The tears she'd fought since hearing her mother's voice built behind her eyes, choking her. The hope that had burned so brightly in her heart only a matter of hours earlier now seemed the musing of an overoptimistic fool.

She squeezed her eyes shut, a single tear easing from the corner of her eye and rolling down her cheek. Why had her mother come back into her life? Why now, when she and Hayes had rediscovered each other? Why when she had been feeling so confident and capable? When she had so much to prove to him?

It was as if her past had popped up to mock her for her feelings of self-worth and self-confidence.

Acknowledging exhaustion, Alice pushed away from the door. Tomorrow, she would call Maggie. Her perpetually positive foster mother had always had the ability to bring her out of herself, had always provided an understanding and loving shoulder.

Yes, Maggie would help her put her mother's reappearance into perspective. Because of her own background, Maggie would understand Alice's feelings better than anyone else.

Soothed by the thought of talking to her foster mother, Alice headed for bed.

Alice didn't call Maggie the next day or the next. Every time she picked up the phone, she found an excuse not to mention her mother's call. It was almost as if, in her heart of hearts, she believed that if she ignored the situation, it would go away.

Her feelings of uncertainty over her and Hayes's relationship didn't go away. If anything, in the days and weeks that passed since that evening at her house, Alice's sense of fatalism grew. She and Hayes continued to see each other, continued to be lovers, yet their time together lacked emotional intimacy.

Hayes distanced himself from her, and she felt that distance keenly. Physically they were as close as two people could be, yet in almost every other way a wall separated them, solid and impenetrable. And the wall seemed to grow every day.

Alice stood in a patch of sunlight that tumbled through her kitchen window. She checked her watch, acknowledging that she and Sheri would be late, but also that it didn't really matter.

She turned away from the sunny window. Hayes never talked about his feelings for her—if indeed he had any—never talked about the future, never of love.

Because they had no future together. Because he didn't love her.

He never would.

Alice flexed her fingers in frustration. Every moment she and Hayes spent together reminded her of past moments spent together. She sensed in him an almost trapped feeling, like a cornered animal searching desperately for a way out of its predicament.

She'd sensed the same thing in him twelve years ago, right before she'd lost the baby and he had ended their relationship.

It was only a matter of time before he ended it again.

With a sigh, she crossed to the kitchen table and the bouquet of spring blossoms at its center. She touched one of the petals with her fingertip. Dewy and soft. Fragile. The way she felt when she was with Hayes.

She dropped her hand. When together, she'd let him know nothing of her feelings; she'd kept their encounters light and unemotional.

It had been the hardest thing she'd ever done. She longed to talk to him, longed to lean on him. To cry and cling and beg.

She longed for his love.

She would never have it.

"I'm almost ready," Sheri called from the other room. "All I have left to do is my hair."

"No problem," Alice answered. "I'll be on the front porch."

She walked to the front door, out onto the porch, and crossed to the railing. There she lifted her face to the sun. Spring had finally burst into full bloom. The scents and colors of Louisiana in April were everywhere, rich and brilliant; in a matter of days the temperature had gone from pleasant to seasonably warm.

She and Sheri were going to Maggie's for lunch; her foster mother planned to regale them with an account of her and her husband's second honeymoon trip to Paris. Alice smiled. When they'd talked the other day, Maggie had sounded like a love-struck teenager. Royce Adler had to be the most romantic man in the world. And the one most in love with his wife.

Alice's smile faded. She wanted what Maggie and Royce had. She wanted it with Hayes.

Tears gathered behind her eyes and she fought them off. She wasn't certain she wanted to discuss her problems with Maggie. She didn't want Maggie to worry; she didn't want to dampen Maggie's excitement over her and Royce's trip. She wasn't even certain she wanted advice.

Alice curved her hands around the wooden porch railing. Her mother had phoned several times since that first call, but luckily she hadn't been home any of the times and the answering machine had picked up. She'd never returned the calls and that made her feel both cowardly and mean spirited.

The truth was, she didn't want to deal with this. She didn't want to face it.

"Ready."

Alice turned. The teenager wore a pretty peach-colored maternity outfit they had picked out together the day before. Alice smiled. "You look lovely."

Sheri lowered her gaze. "Thanks."

The teenager said it as if she didn't believe the compliment had been sincere. Alice frowned. She had noticed Sheri taking a lot of extra time with her appearance lately. It was almost as if she felt like she needed help to look pretty, now that her pregnancy was showing.

Alice studied the girl from the corner of her eye as they started for the car. The past few weeks Sheri hadn't been happy. Her mood had been subdued, her spirits flagging. Alice hoped visiting Maggie and the kids would lift Sheri's spirits as well as her own.

Sheri's pregnancy was not going well. She fluctuated between feeling energetic and feeling fatigued and nauseated. Ultrasounds had shown that the baby was not growing as quickly as it should, although Dr. Bennett had assured them that not every fetus grew at exactly the same rate. But the doctor was concerned enough that she had prescribed fifty percent bed rest, a minimum of stress and no major physical exertion.

Yet more than the troublesome pregnancy was dampening Sheri's spirits, Alice knew. In fact, she suspected that the stress and uncertainty of the situation was causing some of Sheri's physical discomfort.

They climbed into the car and buckled their safety belts. Alice smiled reassuringly at Sheri. "You okay?"

"I feel fine."

Which didn't answer her question. Alice ached at the sadness in Sheri's eyes and wished the girl would open up to her, but for now, she wouldn't push. "Good. Let's go."

During the drive to Maggie's, Sheri didn't speak. Alice attempted to make conversation, but the teenager refused to be drawn out. Instead she sat with her gaze turned to the side window, worrying her bottom lip.

When they reached Maggie's they were greeted by the sound of children laughing. They stepped out of the car, having to maneuver around a half a dozen bikes and a big red wagon.

Josh, Maggie's eight-year-old, caught sight of them first. He broke free of the group of equally exuberant and sweaty little boys he was playing with and bounded toward her, his face wreathed in a brilliant smile.

"Aunt Alice!"

She answered his smile, squatted and held out her arms. He launched himself into them.

She hugged him tightly, breathing in his little-boy smell, loving him so much she ached. "I've missed you so much. You look like you've grown a foot in these past few weeks."

He scowled. "Manda calls me 'shrimp.' And I don't like it."

She had no doubts about that. She ruffled his blond hair.

"Someday you'll be able to call her 'shrimp.' I promise. Just wait."

He narrowed his eyes speculatively, obviously planning his revenge.

Alice hugged him again, then dropped her arms. "I bet you're glad to have your folks home."

"Oh, yeah. They brought me a neat model of the Eiffel Tower. It even has an elevator." He wrinkled his nose. "But they only brought Manda a funny hat."

"That 'funny hat' is a beret," Amanda announced, coming up beside them. She stopped and, with all the sophistication and dignity her thirteen-and-a-half-year-old self could muster, looked down her nose at her brother. "All real artists have them."

"Then why'd they bring you one?"

He stuck out his tongue and Amanda took a threatening step toward her brother. "You'd better watch it, shrimp, or I'll—"

Hoping to avoid a full-scale war, Alice stood and hugged Amanda. She touched her long, dark hair. "You look more like your mother every time I see you."

"Quit insultin' my mom," Josh shouted gleefully, earning a glare from his sister.

After the siblings had verbally tussled a few more moments, Alice introduced them to Sheri, then started toward the house, where they told her Maggie waited.

The other woman met them at the door, smiling warmly. She held it open. "Was that my kids I heard bickering?"

"Who else's?" Alice kissed Maggie's cheek.

Maggie sighed. "I'm afraid one of these days I'll find them rolling on the ground, beating each other senseless."

"Josh is waiting until he gets a little bigger. He wants an unfair advantage." At Maggie's look, Alice laughed. "They adore each other, and you know it."

Maggie smiled. "I know. I just wish they'd do it a little more civilly." She turned her gaze and smile on Sheri, and held out a hand. "You must be Sheri. I've heard so many wonderful things about you. Come in. Lunch is ready."

Toys were strewn from one end of the elegant old house to the other, and Maggie smiled ruefully. "Excuse our mess. It seems we've become the neighborhood hangout."

Alice laughed. "And you love it."

Maggie grinned and leaned conspiratorially toward Sheri. "She's right, crazy as it seems. I'd hate it if my children wanted to play at somebody else's house. What would I do with all the quiet?''

Maggie had fixed shrimp salad stuffed in Creole tomatoes. She served the salads with crusty French bread and sweet green grapes. They ate out on the sun porch, and through lunch, Maggie told them about her and Royce's trip.

As the meal progressed, Sheri became more and more animated. Alice watched the teenager and smiled. Sheri didn't realize it, but she was under the influence of that special Maggie magic. Her foster mother worked it on everyone, from the very young to the ancient, the rich to the poor, conservative to liberal. No one could be around Maggie Ryan Adler and not feel as if bathed in sunshine.

When they finished lunch—topping the salads off with a slice of Maggie's award-winning and sinfully rich chocolate cake—the children came barreling in, demanding giant slices of the cake and ending up stealing Sheri away for a game of Monopoly.

Delighted to spend time alone with Maggie, Alice helped her clear the table. Those quiet moments were like old times, comfortable and reassuring. Everything good in her life, the positive feelings she had about herself and other people, were all on account of Maggie's love.

Alice set the last plate in the sink and turned to Maggie. "I need to tell you something."

Maggie looked up, immediately concerned, ready to do battle for her charge. She searched Alice's gaze. "By your tone, it sounds serious."

"My... mother has contacted me. She wants to see me."

Maggie set the plate she held in her hands carefully back in the sink. "Your mother...wants to see you? After all these years?"

"Yes." Alice slipped her hands into her trouser pockets, hating the way they trembled. "My dad died. A couple of months ago."

"I'm sorry."

Alice lifted her shoulders. "Don't be. He was neither a good father nor a sterling example of humanity."

"No, he wasn't." Maggie let out a long breath. "And now that she's alone, she wants to reconnect with her only child."

"So she said."

For long moments Maggie remained silent. Then she cleared her throat. "What do you want, Alice?"

"Truthfully?" Maggie nodded. "I want her to go away. I want my life to return to the way it was."

"Have you told her that?"

"No." Alice pulled her hands out of her pockets and twisted her fingers together, feeling young, uncertain and apologetic. "It's just that...it's hard, you know. It's...I feel like a bad daughter for not wanting to see her. She wants to pick up where we left off. I feel like I should—"

Bright spots of angry color tinted Maggie's cheeks. "And exactly where is it she thinks you left off? When she was making your life a living hell?" Maggie took a deep breath and held up her hands. "I'm sorry, this is your decision, but it makes me so angry. I'll try to be impartial—"

Alice made a sound that was part sob, part laugh. "No, don't. Be as biased as you want. Everybody needs a champion."

"Oh, Alice." Maggie crossed to her and put her arms around her. "I'm sorry this happened."

Alice hugged her back, almost fiercely. "Maybe she's changed. Maybe I should give her the benefit of the doubt. After all, I'm in the business of personal change. It can happen."

Maggie brushed Alice's bangs away from her face. "You don't have to see her, you know. You're not under any moral obligation."

"That's the problem. I'm not so sure that's true." She drew in a shuddering breath, battling for control. "Besides, I'm not sure she'll give up until I do see her."

"I don't want you hurt."

"I know." Alice drew a deep breath and shifted her gaze to the glass-walled sun room and the riotous spring garden beyond. "There's something else, Maggie." She turned and met her foster mother's eyes. "I'm involved with someone."

"Involved?" she repeated, her eyes sparkling. "Like a relationship?"

"I guess." Alice looked down at her hands. She couldn't bring herself to tell Maggie that the man she was involved with was the same one who had broken her heart twelve years before. Maggie had seen her through that heartache and she would never understand. Just as she had never forgiven Hayes. "Yes."

"But that's...wonderful." Maggie frowned. "Isn't it?"

"It could be. I mean... I'm in love with..." Tears flooded her eyes, and she blinked them back, feeling like an idiot. "I'm in love with him, but I'm afraid it's... not going to work out. He's not a commitment kind of man."

"But if you love each oth—"

"I said I love him. He doesn't love me."

Maggie straightened. "Then he's an idiot." At Alice's look, she frowned. "I mean it. If he's so stupid and blind that he can't see what a prize you are, he isn't worth having."

"You know I don't believe that."

"I know." Maggie crossed to her, stopping directly in front of her. She looked her in the eye. "But you should. I want you to think about it, Alice." Maggie searched her expression. "Promise me you will."

As she opened her mouth to do just that, Royce arrived home and all hell broke loose. Manda and Josh, squealing at the tops of their lungs, threw themselves at their father. With an imitation war whoop, he grabbed them both and carried them to the kitchen, Josh over a shoulder and Manda under an arm.

When he reached the kitchen, the laughing children were dumped unceremoniously on the floor, then Royce spun Maggie into his arms and kissed her soundly.

Watching them, pangs of longing speared through her, so poignant Alice caught her breath. She wanted what Maggie and Royce had. It was all she'd ever wanted.

She wanted it with Hayes.

The remainder of her visit passed quickly. Alice collected Sheri and said her goodbyes. At the door, Maggie hugged her tightly. "Think about what I said, okay?"

Alice agreed, and moments later, she and Sheri were on their way home. The ride from Maggie's proved even quieter than the one there. Subdued, Sheri refused to speak. She stared out the window, her expression tight and unhappy. Alice drew her eyebrows together. Sheri had seemed to have a good time at Maggie's. She had smiled and laughed and joined in the general ruckus.

Now the teenager seemed sad to the point of depressed. Alice reached across the seat and touched Sheri's arm. "Want to talk about it?"

Sheri glanced at her from the corner of her eye, then looked away. "Talk about what?"

"You tell me. Something's got you down."

Sheri folded her hands in her lap. "It's...nothing."

The light ahead turned yellow and Alice slowed to a stop. She turned to Sheri. "Right. And pigs fly."

For several moments Sheri remained silent, then she let out a long, angry breath. "It just hurts, that's all."

"What hurts?"

"Seeing them. Maggie, Royce and their kids. They're so...happy." Her voice cracked, and she cleared her throat. "They really love each other."

Alice's eyes misted. She understood exactly what Sheri referred to. "Yeah, they do."

"It's just that...it's what I..."

Alice waited. She saw Sheri battling for control, battling for indifference. She lost the battle. "It's what I always wanted," she whispered. "It's the family I always...dreamed of."

A horn blared behind them, and Alice started through the intersection. "I know how you feel," she said softly. "It's the one I always dreamed of, too."

Sheri laid a hand over her abdomen, rubbing gently. "How come some people have so much and others...don't have anything?"

"It doesn't seem fair, does it?"

Sheri shook her head. "That's all I ever wanted. To be loved." She turned her swimming gaze to Alice. "Is that so much to ask? Am I so selfish for wanting that?"

Alice thought of her own bereft childhood, thought of the way she had longed for affection and approval from her parents. She shook her head, her chest tight. "No, it's not too much. Love should be every child's birthright. But sometimes, something goes terribly wrong. The only thing we can try to do is right that something."

"Bet they never had anything to try to right," she murmured bitterly. "Bet they were born to all that happiness."

Alice shook her head. "That's not true. Neither of them had an ideal childhood, and in fact, Maggie's mother abandoned Maggie when she was five. She was lucky. A wonderful family took her in."

"The way Maggie took you in."

"Yes." Alice turned a corner, inching her way down a street filled with playing children. "Maggie and Royce's marriage has had its bumpy times—that's for sure. They really had to work at staying together. In fact, they almost divorced. Adopting Amanda brought them back together."

Sheri looked at Alice in shocked surprise. "Amanda is adopted?"

"So is Josh." Alice smiled at the teenager's expression. "Did you think adopted kids were different than others? Did you think you could pick them out from a lineup or something?"

"No. It's just that... Maggie and Royce love them so much. You would think, you know, that they're really theirs."

"They are really theirs," Alice said softly. "There's only one difference between a biological child and an adopted one, Sheri. And it has nothing to do with love."

Sheri frowned and rubbed her abdomen again. "How come they had to adopt?"

"Maggie and Royce wanted children. They wanted to share their lives with children. They wanted to be *parents*. Maggie couldn't conceive."

"Not at all?" Sheri drew her eyebrows together. "Wow. Sad."

"It was. Until the day Amanda came into their lives. Then it didn't matter anymore."

As if mulling over what Alice had said, Sheri leaned her head against the seat back and closed her eyes. She remained that way until, moments later, Alice pulled the car to a stop in front of her cottage and cut off the engine.

Without speaking, they both alighted from the vehicle and started up the sidewalk to the house. When they reached the front door, Sheri caught her arm, her grip almost painful.

Surprised, Alice looked at her. "What is it, Sheri?"

"You've got to help me, Miss A. I don't know what to do."

Alice covered the girl's hand. In her eyes she saw a kind of desperation. "I will if I can. Tell me what's bothering you."

Sheri drew in a deep, shaky breath. "I'm afraid everything is going to go wrong. I think it already has."

"What do you mean? Your pregnancy?"

She shook her head, tears flooding her eyes. "Me and Jeff. Our plans." The tears spilled down her cheeks. "I don't think Jeff's happy about our getting married. He says he is . . . but . . ." Sheri bit her lip.

Alice drew her eyebrows together. "But what?"

"He's acting funny. Preoccupied and moody. He's cutting school. And this thing with his dad . . . it never used to be so bad." She pushed at the tears on her cheeks. "He's changed. The way he feels about me has changed. I don't know, but I see something in his eyes, something—"

Trapped. Hunted. The way Hayes had looked all those years ago. Alice's chest tightened even as she smoothed a hand reassuringly over Sheri's hair. "That's what's been bothering you, isn't it?"

Sheri nodded, and Alice's heart went out to the girl. She understood her feelings; she ached for her.

"I want us to be happy," Sheri whispered. "Like Maggie and Royce. I want our baby to be happy."

She started to cry in earnest, and Alice drew her gently into her arms, stroking her back and murmuring sounds of comfort and support. "You need to talk to him, Sheri. Don't assume he doesn't love you anymore. Don't assume he doesn't want you or the baby. Maybe he's just scared."

Sheri sniffed. "You really think so?"

"I think it's a good bet. And talking to him certainly beats the alternative." She drew back and met Sheri's gaze. "Doesn't it?"

A smile tugged at Sheri's mouth. "I think I'll go call him now. Is that okay?"

Alice nodded and opened the front door. She watched the teenager race to the phone, looking happy and hopeful for the first time in days. She smiled. She had this feeling about Sheri and Jeff, that they were going to make it. That they were meant to be together.

Unlike her and Hayes. Her smile faded. She thought of Hayes, of their relationship and of Maggie's words. *If he's too stupid and blind not to see what a prize you are, then he's not worth having.* If only she could believe that. If only she didn't want him enough for the both of them.

Something had to give. Or someone. Their relationship couldn't continue without change.

But not yet. She clenched her hands. She couldn't bear the thought of going on without him. For now, she would take the moments of happiness he offered. They would be enough.

Chapter Eleven

Hayes stood at his office window and gazed out at downtown New Orleans. Twenty stories below, the St. Charles Avenue streetcar rumbled past, cars jockeyed for position in the five o'clock race out of the central business district and a dizzying assortment of humanity hurried past. In stark contrast, his leather-and-mahogany-outfitted office resounded with the quiet.

A light rain had been falling all day, and the drizzle and gray sky combined to make the hour seem later, his gloomy mood blacker. Hayes frowned. He hadn't called Alice in two days, although in those two days he'd picked up the phone at least a hundred times to do so. He hadn't driven by her place or Hope House, even though he'd thought about doing so constantly.

Hayes gazed out at the drizzle, wishing for a ray of

sunshine, acknowledging that Alice's smile stole over him like sunshine, warm and brilliant.

He drew his eyebrows together. What was going on with her? With them? The past two days of silence had been mutual. She hadn't contacted him; she hadn't tried.

Was it over between them already? Before it had hardly begun?

His chest tight, he swung away from the window. She'd told him she didn't expect anything from him, had guaranteed no emotional complications. She'd been true to her word.

Hayes flexed his fingers. She didn't feel the same about him as she had twelve years ago. She didn't feel as strongly. He told himself her emotional ambivalence toward him was good. He told himself the relationship was better off without the complication, the confusion, of love.

But he hated it. Just as he hated the wall he felt between them, the emotional distance. He felt as if she held her emotions in check when with him, as if she kept a part of herself hidden from him.

He wanted the Alice he had known twelve years ago, the one who had loved and needed him. He missed her. He had for years.

Hayes snorted with self-derision. He was a sorry bastard. No doubt about it. On the one hand he wanted her at arm's length, on the other he longed to pull her closer, longed to make her see how much he meant to her. What a jerk he was; he wanted everything from her, even though he had nothing to offer in return.

Hayes pressed the heels of his hands to his eyes. He missed her. So much that it had been nearly impossible to concentrate on work, sleep had eluded him and he'd barked at everyone and anyone who had dared approach him.

His secretary poked her head into the office. "I'm going now, Hayes. You need anything before I do?"

He looked over his shoulder at her. "No, Susan. I'll see you in the morning."

"Tomorrow's Saturday," she chided. "Jeff has a ball game. You're taking a date. And you're going to have fun." She shook her head. "Let me amend that. Please have fun. I don't think I can take another week of working for an ill-tempered grizzly."

He forced a smile. "I'll see what I can do. Now, go on. You'll miss your ride."

Rain splattered the window, and he scowled at it. He'd forgotten about Jeff's ball game, had forgotten that he and Alice had made plans to go with Sheri to watch it.

Tomorrow he would see Alice. He sucked in a quick, sharp breath, acknowledging the way that made him feel. Happy. Expectant. Hopeful.

Like a total jackass.

Hayes swore. His relationship with Alice was out of control. It had been since the night he'd seen her with a knife pressed to her throat. He shook his head. Whom was he trying to kid? It had been out of control since the morning he'd walked into her office and seen her for the first time in twelve years.

Swearing again, he swung away from the window. He'd allowed himself to become too involved with her. He'd allowed his emotions to overrule his head, had allowed himself to forget what kind of man he was. And what kind of woman she was, what she needed to survive and flourish.

He would never be able to make her happy.

And he couldn't bear to make her unhappy.

Hayes crossed to his desk. He pulled open the top right drawer and took out a photograph buried under some papers. Taking in a deep, fortifying breath, he gazed at it. The photo showed him and Isabel shortly after their marriage. In it they were both smiling. Real smiles. Happy ones. Isabel looked bright and eager; he looked like a man who believed in happily-ever-after, like a man with a million illusions.

He drew his eyebrows together, his chest tight and aching. He kept the photo not because he still loved or longed for Isabel or because he still mourned. He kept it as a reminder of how badly he could fail at a relationship. A reminder of just how unhappy he could make someone.

And to remind him of how out of his depth he was when it came to the world of emotions.

Hayes smoothed the film of dust off the photo's glass. The picture had been taken only fifteen years earlier. It seemed a lifetime ago, more even. He cocked his head, eyes narrowed. Had he really been that smiling young man? Had he really been so carefree? It seemed impossible to him now.

He tightened his fingers on the brass frame, the truth rocking through him. Except when with Alice. She made him feel the way he had all those years ago; she made him believe in happy endings.

And that scared the hell out of him, because he knew their relationship wouldn't last.

He drew in another deep, steadying breath. How had he allowed himself to become entangled with her again? How could he have been so self-indulgent? So selfish?

Hayes took one last, hard look at the photo, dropped it back into the drawer, then snapped it shut. The longer he let this charade continue, the more Alice would be hurt. And the more he would miss her when she was gone.

Gone. A lifetime without Alice. A lifetime of flat gray days and nights, a lifetime without warmth.

That was what these two days had been about, he realized. He'd been testing himself. For what, he wasn't sure. But even so, he hadn't a doubt that he'd failed. Miserably.

How could he have won? If he had, wouldn't he feel jubilation instead of this gray nothingness?

His phone rang, interrupting his thoughts. He picked it up. "Hayes Bradford."

"Mr. Bradford, I'm glad I caught you before you left for the day. This is Nancy Walker, Jeff's principal at Mandeville High."

"Yes, Dr. Walker. What can I do for you?"

The woman hesitated, and Hayes knew he was in for an unpleasant conversation. "I'm calling about Jeff, of course. And I must tell you, I never thought I would be making this kind of call about your son. He's always been a model student."

Hayes tightened his grip on the receiver. "Until now, I take it."

"I'm afraid so. I'll be blunt, Mr. Bradford. Jeff has been missing a lot of classes. And when he does attend, he's neither prepared nor attentive. He's failing to turn in assignments and flunking his exams. We've sent several notices home and left messages on your machine, but I suspect you haven't gotten them."

Anger at his son's duplicity thundered through Hayes; he fought to hold on to it. "No," he said tightly. "I haven't."

"At first we thought his absences were the result of genuine illnesses. He brought excuses from home each time. But after so many absences without our speaking directly to you, we began to suspect—"

"How long has this been going on?"

"Three weeks."

"And you're just calling me now?"

"As I explained—"

"Of course." Hayes cleared his throat. "I apologize if I sound gruff, but as I'm sure you know, this is not the kind of news a father wants to hear."

"Jeff's been banned from playing in tomorrow's game because of his grades. He won't be allowed to play again until he raises them."

Hayes swore silently. Jeff had never had any trouble with school; he'd always been an A student. "Does Jeff know about the game?"

"His coach talked to him first thing this morning." The principal drew in a deep breath. "Is something going on in Jeff's life that we should know about? The counselor here has tried to talk with him, as has his coach and a few of his teachers. But he refuses to be drawn into any kind of a conversation. In fact, he's been sullen and uncommunicative. Which is also unlike Jeff. I'd hoped you could shed some light on Jeff's state of mind."

Could he? Hayes wondered. Did he have even a glimmer of understanding about what his son felt? What motivated him? He shook his head. If he did he wouldn't be standing here feeling stunned and betrayed and totally in the dark.

"Perhaps I could come in for a conference Monday or Tuesday?" He flipped open his appointment book. "I could meet you Monday late afternoon or before ten on Tuesday."

"Monday afternoon would be fine. Will four o'clock work for you?"

"Four o'clock will be fine," Hayes said, checking his watch, thinking instead of how long it would take him to get across the causeway and home, wondering what he would to say to his son when he got there. "I'll see you then, Dr. Walker. Goodbye."

Hayes flew across the causeway, making it to the north shore in record time. He swung into his driveway and slammed out of the car. Jeff's Mazda sat in its usual spot and Hayes took a deep breath, battling to hold on to his anger. Nothing would be solved if he went in shouting.

He stalked up the walk and let himself inside. Jeff had tossed his car keys on the entryway table; Hayes scooped them up and dropped them into his jacket pocket.

He heard the sound of the television and followed it. Jeff sat slouched on the sofa, staring blankly at a music video. Hayes crossed to the set, flicked it off and swung to face his son.

"Your principal called today." Jeff met his eyes. Hayes thought he looked a little pale. "I hear you're not playing tomorrow."

The boy jutted his chin out. "That's right."

"I also hear you've been cutting class. I hear you're not turning in your homework, and that your grades have slipped."

Jeff arched his eyebrows, the picture of cocky arrogance. "If Dr. Walker called, I guess you have heard that."

Hayes worked to control his temper. "We need to talk."

Jeff shrugged. "If you insist."

Jeff had never been a smart aleck, had never been one of those children who affected a breezy, know-it-all air. That he was now, at eighteen, was as disturbing as it was infuriating.

Hayes counted to ten. Then twenty. "Do you realize how messing up now can affect the rest of your life? You can blow your entire senior year by continuing to do what you've been doing. Is that what you want? If you flunk out this year, even if you make up the courses in summer school, those grades stay on your records. Forever, Jeff."

The teenager shrugged. "What does it matter? I'm not going to Georgetown. The state schools will take me."

Hayes shook his head, taking a step toward his son. "My God, Jeff, are you deliberately trying to ruin your life?"

"I thought I already had," Jeff shot back. "According to you, marrying Sheri is accomplishing that." He arched his eyebrows in exaggerated disbelief. "That's possible? You can ruin a life twice? In the same year?"

Hayes's tenuous hold on his temper snapped. "You're grounded. You go to school—you come home. That's it."

Jeff jumped to his feet, hands clenched, jaw tight with fury. "You can't ground me! I'm eighteen years old."

"Like hell I can't." Hayes pulled Jeff's car keys out of his pocket. "You'll get them back when you prove to me you deserve your own wheels. Until then, I'll drive you to school and arrange for someone to pick you up."

"This is just a way to keep me and Sheri apart."

Anger exploded inside Hayes. "This doesn't have a damn thing to do with Sheri! This has to do with you. Lying to me. Hiding the truth. Shirking your responsibilities."

"I live up to my responsibilities. Can you say the same?"

Hayes took another step toward his son, then another, stopping when they were nose to nose. In his son's expression he saw reflected back at him his own fury and unwillingness to bend.

His own desperation.

Hayes gazed at his son, the truth of that worming through his anger, touching a place deep inside him. He reached a hand out to Jeff. "What do you want from me? What do you want me to do? To say?"

For one slim moment, Jeff's expression twisted with pain, then he visibly pulled himself together, squaring his shoulders, cocking up his chin. "I don't want anything from you. Nothing."

Hayes searched his son's expression, looking for a glimmer of what he'd seen only a moment ago. Looking for a glimmer of the boy he had been, the happy boy who had loved and looked up to him. "What's happened to you?" he asked softly. "I don't even recognize you anymore."

"What does it matter to you?" Jeff shot back, his voice thick. "You've never been interested in me."

Hayes took an involuntary step backward, stunned. His son couldn't have hurt him more if he'd laid into him with his fists. "That's not true, Jeff. I've always been interested. You're my son."

"And that's supposed to mean something?"

"It means everything." Hayes swallowed. "Who are you trying to punish, Jeff? Me? Or yourself?"

Jeff started to walk away; Hayes caught his arm. "Talk to me. Tell me what's going on with you."

For a moment Jeff wavered. Hayes saw his hesitation, his indecision. Saw in that fraction of a second what he'd been longing to see—a flash of the boy Jeff had once been. Then that boy was gone, replaced by the angry young man he had become.

Jeff jerked his arm free. "Talk to you so you can punish me some more? So you can tell me how badly I'm screwing up. No thanks, *Dad*. As I see it, we have nothing to talk about."

Hayes stiffened against Jeff's verbal blows. "I want you to be happy. That's *all* I want. If you feel you need to do this thing, I'll stand by you. I'll support you in whatever decision you make."

Jeff jerked his chin up, narrowing his eyes. "What's that supposed to mean?"

"I'll pay for Georgetown. I'll help support you and Sheri."

For a full ten seconds Jeff stared at him, obviously nonplussed. Then he shook his head. "I don't get it, Dad. What's the point? Do you want me to owe you? Do you want me to be grateful?"

Hurt overpowered Hayes; he fought to keep the pain from showing. "Has it gotten so bad between us that I can't do this for you? So bad that you can't believe I just might want you to be happy?"

Jeff shook his head again. "You taught me that a man stands on his own two feet. That a man is strong for his family. I'm not going to take your money. I don't want it. I don't need it. And I don't want to owe you anything. Sheri and I can make it on our own."

Hayes caught himself starting to tell Jeff what a big mistake he was making, then swallowed the words. Instead he gazed at his son, his chest heavy and tight. He'd never felt so at a loss, so out of his depth. He wanted to reach out to his son, longed to tell him something, anything, that would make it better for him. He held out a hand. "Please, Jeff. Help me help you."

Jeff shrugged off his father's hand and took a step away. He met Hayes's eyes evenly. "It's too late. Just too damn late."

Hayes watched Jeff walk away, and felt his heart breaking.

He'd lost his son.

Alice glanced at the phone beside her bed for the third time in thirty minutes. She'd been so certain Hayes would call. He'd been on her mind all afternoon and evening, and now, at nearly midnight, he was still on her mind. So much so, she hadn't been able to sleep.

She set aside her novel and leaned her head back against the propped-up pillows. He'd been busy; so had she. They'd made no special plans; there'd been no special reason he should have called.

But he should have called anyway. They were lovers. When they were together, they shared the most intimate part of themselves.

She rubbed her temple, at the headache that throbbed there. Hayes's silence had been unnatural. It had been ripe with meaning. She had interpreted it a dozen different ways, all bad.

Sighing, she dropped her hand. And what of herself? She'd picked up the phone a dozen times, intending to call him, to break the silence by saying hello or demanding to know what was going on. But each time, her pride had overruled her desire to speak with him.

It was the beginning of the end.

The truth of that hit her squarely in the gut, stealing her breath, the last of her hopeful illusions. She'd known all along that she and Hayes wouldn't last; she'd known he didn't love her, that he never would. She'd felt his distance, his second thoughts, from the beginning.

Still she'd allowed herself to believe in something that wasn't there. That would never be there. She'd put on blinders and happily gone her way.

Happily. Her eyes filled with tears. When she'd been with him, she'd been happy. Deliriously so. It had felt right between them. It had felt as though it would last.

Calling herself a ninny, she brushed at the tears on her cheeks. So she'd allowed herself to pretend. She'd allowed herself to believe in the future. Had allowed herself to believe in a happily-ever-after with Hayes.

Now it was over.

"Miss A.!" Sheri stumbled into her room, her arms curved around her middle, her expression panicked. "Something's wrong!"

An ugly dark stain spread across the front of Sheri's nightgown. Alice stared at it, horror dawning inside her. Throwing off the covers, she jumped out of bed and raced to Sheri's side.

"I woke up and..." The teenager fought for breath. "It hurt and I...it felt so...wet."

She took the girl's arm. "Come. I want you to sit down while I call Dr. Bennett."

Sheri caught her arm, clutching at her. "You've got to help me, Miss A.! Please. I don't want my baby to die."

"Calm down," Alice murmured, fighting to stay calm herself. "We're going to call Dr. Bennett, then head to the emergency room."

"I'm bleeding." She lifted her gaze to Alice's. "I can't stop bleeding."

"I know, sweetie." And she did know. She remembered, so vividly it took her breath. She eased the teenager gently onto the edge of the bed, then pried Sheri's cold fingers from around her arm. "I'll be right back."

"Don't leave me." Sheri caught Alice's hands. "I'm scared."

Alice squeezed the teenager's fingers. "I know. But I have to call Dr. Bennett. You're going to be all right. Just hold on."

"I want Jeff," she whispered, her eyes swimming, her expression bleak. "Call Jeff."

Alice nodded. "As soon as I phone Dr. Bennett."

Sheri dropped her hands and sagged rag doll-like, curling her arms around herself.

As quickly as she could, Alice found Sheri a clean gown and some sanitary pads, then grabbed several bath towels from the linen closet. From the bedroom she heard Sheri's whimpers, mewls not of pain but of despair.

Alice's heart turned over. If only she didn't understand how Sheri felt. If only she didn't fear that it was already too late.

She shook herself. Just because she'd lost her baby didn't mean Sheri would lose hers. Sheri was young. And healthy. In the twelve years since she herself had miscarried the advances in medical technology had been staggering.

They would be able to save Sheri's baby, she thought grimly. Everything was going to be all right.

Holding on to that hope, Alice phoned the doctor. As she expected, Dr. Bennett told her to take Sheri directly to Saint Mary's emergency room. Hanging up, she took a deep breath and dialed Hayes's number. He answered immediately, but she'd awakened him—she could tell by his thick, sleepy voice.

For a moment she couldn't find her voice. She felt choked, impotent. In that one moment she felt nineteen again and helpless to stop the loss of the life inside her.

She had wanted her baby, her little girl, so much.

"Hello?" he said again. "Is anyone there?"

She cleared her throat. "Hayes, it's Alice. There's no time to talk. Sheri and I are heading to the emergency room. I think she might be . . . it doesn't look good. She's going to need Jeff."

For a fraction of a second he said nothing, and she wondered if he'd even heard her. "Hayes, are you—"

"We'll be there," he said tightly, then hung up.

Alice stared at the phone for a moment, hurt spearing through her. She hadn't spoken to him in two days. And just now his voice had been devoid of warmth, devoid of emotion.

He felt nothing for her.

Hands shaking so badly she feared she wouldn't be able to drive, she dropped the phone back onto the receiver and hurried back to Sheri. She found the girl exactly as she'd left her, hugging herself, bent over in pain.

"Jeff's on his way," she said quickly. "So is Dr. Bennett. They'll meet us at the emergency room." Alice handed her the fresh gown and pads. "Put these on. I'll help you."

Sheri lifted her gaze to Alice's. Alice saw every one of her own fears, past and present, mirrored back at her. "Promise me, Miss A. Promise me I won't lose my baby."

She wanted to reassure Sheri, wished she could more than anything in the world. But she couldn't say the words because she didn't believe them. She covered Sheri's trembling hand with her own. "Dr. Bennett is really good. She's going to do everything she can."

Alice helped Sheri change, then helped her to the car. She drove the winding roads to the interstate faster than she ever had before and, when she reached the highway, accelerated to a speed that left her breathless.

Alice cut Sheri a glance from the corner of her eye. The teenager huddled in the seat, her robe drawn tightly around her. She looked so young. So vulnerable. Her heart turned over. "Just a couple of more minutes. You're going to be fine."

Sheri started to cry then, the tears slipping silently down her cheeks. "I don't want to lose my baby. But I am, aren't I, Miss A.?"

Alice swallowed past the lump in her throat. "We don't know that, Sheri. Nothing's certain yet."

"I want her to live. So bad I..." She twisted her fingers in her lap. "I want her to hunt Easter eggs and go to first grade and wear a pink dress with lots of bows and ruffles."

Alice tightened her fingers on the wheel. She'd had wishes like that once. She had dreamed of a daughter and a too-frilly dress. A beautiful child who would love her without reservation. She swallowed hard.

"I never had a dress like that," Sheri continued, wiping at the tears on her cheeks. "But I remember seeing one in a window downtown. And I remember gazing at it and thinking that someday...when I had a little girl..."

The teenager drew in a quick, pained breath, and Alice reached across the seat and covered her clasped hands. "Hold on to that thought, Sheri. It's a really nice one."

She curved her fingers around Alice's. Sheri's were as cold as ice, and Alice fought back her alarm. "I want...her...to have a good life. A happy life."

"I know, sweetie." Tears choked her, and Alice cleared her throat. "You'll be a good mother. I know you will."

Sheri shook her head. "I'm going to...give her up for adoption."

Stunned, Alice took her eyes from the road to look at the teenager. Sheri's expression was determined. She swung her gaze back to the highway. "When did you—"

"After I saw Maggie's kids. After I saw how happy they are and..." Again she shook her head, but this time, Alice knew, in an attempt to ward off tears. "Jeff's not ready to be a parent. I know he loves me and that he wants to do the right thing, but it isn't the right thing. Not for him. He hasn't been happy, not really, since this whole thing started."

Sheri's eyes widened, and she made a sound of pain, squeezing her hands into tight fists. "And I...I want her, but...what do I have to give her?"

"You have love, Sheri. And that's the most important thing of all."

For a long moment Sheri was silent. Then, she turned her tear-soaked eyes to Alice. "That's why I decided to give her up," she whispered. "Because I love her so much. I want her to have parents who'll love her no matter what. Parents who'll think she's the...best thing in the whole world. Parents who won't have any...regrets. And I want her to have that pink dres—"

Again she caught her breath in pain. "Miss A.!"

"I'm hurrying, sweetie. I am. Hold on."

They drove the rest of the way without speaking. Tears trickled down Sheri's cheeks and her lips moved in what Alice suspected was a silent prayer for her baby's life.

Tears built behind Alice's eyes, and she struggled against them, frightened for Sheri, sorry for herself. Twelve years ago she had whispered the same prayer. Only hers hadn't been answered. Her little baby hadn't been meant to be.

She hoped—and prayed—that Sheri and Jeff's little one was meant to be.

She couldn't squelch the fear that it was not.

Chapter Twelve

Within minutes they arrived at Saint Mary's emergency room, and a nurse with a wheelchair rushed out, Jeff and Hayes close behind him. Dr. Bennett arrived on their heels and whisked Sheri into an examining room, leaving the three of them behind to wait. And worry.

Hayes said nothing. As he had their last time there with Sheri, he stood by the window, staring out at the night, his expression tight and unreadable. He seemed lost in his thoughts, unaffected by his surroundings or the impending tragedy.

Didn't he feel anything? Alice wondered, clasping her hands together. Didn't it matter at all to him that he was in danger of losing his grandchild?

She drew in a deep, painful breath. Why should it matter to him? Why should it touch him? It hadn't mattered when he'd lost his own child. Their child.

Pain ripped through her. She'd been such a fool. Such an idiot. Twelve years ago she'd promised herself she would never forget how much Hayes had hurt her. But she had not only forgotten, she had allowed herself to become involved with him again.

And once again, he would hurt her.

The minutes ticked past. She paced. Jeff brooded. The tension in the waiting room thickened with each moment, until Alice found it difficult to breathe. Just as she thought she would scream if they didn't hear something, Dr. Bennett strode into the waiting room, crossing to where Jeff sat. Her expression said it all, and Alice clenched her fingers into fists. *Please, Lord, let it not be true. Please let this baby be safe.*

"I'm sorry." The doctor jammed her hands into the pockets of her white coat, her eyes and voice full of sympathy. "Sheri is fine, but the baby—"

"No." Jeff jumped to his feet, his expression twisted with pain. "No!"

"I'm sorry," the doctor said again. "I know it's small consolation, but I see no reason Sheri won't be able to conceive again. She's young and in good health. This baby... just wasn't meant to be."

Alice brought a hand to her mouth to muffle her own sound of pain. Of grief. Twelve years earlier, her doctor had said those same words to her, in exactly the same way. They had been branded on her soul, and for months afterward she had tried to comfort herself with them.

This baby... just wasn't meant to be.

But those words hadn't comforted her then, and they wouldn't comfort Sheri or Jeff now.

She swung her gaze to Hayes. Although he'd turned his attention to the doctor and Jeff, he hadn't moved from his position at the window, his expression hadn't altered with the news of Sheri and Jeff's loss. Just as his expression hadn't altered all those years ago when he'd heard of their loss.

Hayes hadn't needed comforting. Those words had meant nothing to him.

As if from far away, she heard Jeff ask to see Sheri, heard the doctor give her approval and the two of them leave the room.

Alice didn't shift her gaze from Hayes, his image blurring as her eyes welled with tears. Suddenly she saw the truth. Suddenly she saw what Hayes had been trying to tell her for so long.

He was the wrong man for her. He would never make her happy.

She drew in a quick, tight breath. Hayes would never be there for her. Not the way she needed him to be, not with his heart. He refused to feel. He refused to live by and with his emotions. Whether it had happened with Isabel's death or long before, he'd disconnected himself from his heart.

She shook her head, stunned. He'd seen that so long ago, and yet, until this moment, she hadn't been able to see it.

She hadn't wanted to. Because despite everything, she'd loved him. She loved him still.

Her tears brimmed and spilled over. *If he doesn't love you, he isn't worth having,* Maggie had said. At the time she hadn't believed it. At the time she'd thought she could settle for whatever he had to give her. That being with him would be enough.

She cocked her chin, brushing at the tears on her cheeks. Not any more. She needed love. She needed a man with a whole heart. She needed a man she could cling to. And one who would cling to her.

What a sham their last weeks together had been. She had tried to make him love her by hiding her true feelings. By trying to become like him. It would never work. She could never live a lie.

Hayes turned his gaze to hers, and for long moments they stood unmoving, silently contemplating each other. A muscle worked in his tight jaw; something in his eyes tugged at her heartstrings. She called herself a fool.

He opened his mouth to speak, then closed it and turned back to the window and the deep, dark night. Her heart shattered into a billion pieces. At a time like this, when they should be clinging to each other, when they should be able to share their deepest sorrow, they couldn't even find one word of comfort to exchange.

He couldn't find a word of comfort. She had hundreds, pressing to spill out of her heart and off her tongue. Anger and frustration rushed over her in a hot wave. She wouldn't let him hide.

This time he would know exactly how she felt.

And no matter the outcome, she would know what he did—or didn't—feel for her.

She crossed to where he stood, stopping so close he would have no choice but to look at her. "We need to talk."

Hayes met and searched her gaze, the cold in his tearing at her. "Yes."

She clasped her trembling hands in front of her. "It's not enough, Hayes. I love you, and I can't go on this way."

Except for the slight tightening of his mouth, he didn't move, didn't even seem to breathe. It hurt to look at him, but she forced herself to hold his gaze. "Do you love me? Are you willing to make a commitment to me?"

"Alice, now's not the—"

"The time?" She shook her head. "I think it's the perfect time. Do you love me?"

He hesitated. "I don't want to let you go," he said softly. "I can't...imagine my life without you in it."

Disappointment, so keen she could taste it, spiraled through her. "But that's not love, is it?"

His silence told her more than any words could, and she made a sound of pain. "You don't want to let me go, but you will. Just like that."

"I won't make you happy." He cupped her face in his palms. "I'll want to, but I know what kind of man I am. I know what my strengths are. And my failings."

She covered his hands, discovering they were wet with her own tears. "Why did you come back into my life? Why did you allow me to hope for something more with you?"

"Did I do that, Alice?" He drew his eyebrows together. "I've always been honest with you. Always."

"Have you really?" He tried to draw his hands away, and she tightened her fingers. "Is this what you feel for me? This cold? This emotionless control? Are you showing me everything that's in your heart?"

He laughed, the sound tight and humorless. "Look who's talking about honesty. Have you been honest with me, Alice? All these weeks you've been hiding your feelings from me. How was I supposed to know what was going on inside you? How was I supposed to know what you needed? You told me no emotional complications. You told me you didn't expect anything from our relationship."

She wished she could deny his words, but she couldn't. She hadn't been honest. She dropped her hands and spun away from him. Crossing to the window, she gazed out at the night. "I said those things because they were what you wanted to hear. And because I wanted to be the woman you needed me to be."

"So who's dishonest?"

She didn't turn. "Would it have made a difference if I'd told you, Hayes? Or would it have made you pull even farther and faster away from me?"

"I don't know." He closed the distance between them, stopping directly behind her. He touched her hair lightly. "I never wanted to hurt you."

He eased her against his chest. Beneath her shoulder blade she felt the steady beat of his heart. She squeezed her eyes shut, despair a living thing inside her. "You say that, yet you keep hurting me."

"That's not fair, Alice. And you know it."

"Do I?" She turned and, placing her hands on his chest, tipped her face up to his. "On the way to the hospital, Sheri told me about a little girl's dress, a frilly pink one with ruffles and bows. She dreamed of her daughter wearing it someday." Alice curled her fingers into the soft fleece of his sweatshirt. "I could picture that dress so clearly because I had imagined the same one for our daughter.''

Something moved across his expression, something sad. Something full of regret. He started to pull away from her; she tightened her fingers, stopping him. "If she'd been born, she would have been eleven in March. Do you remember?''

Beneath her hands she felt him stiffen. "I remember.''

"I named her, you know. After Maggie.'' Tears welled in her eyes, and she blinked against them. She wanted to say her piece without crying. She wanted to share her feelings and walk away without breaking down. "To me, she was always little Margaret.''

"You never told me you'd named her,'' he said, his voice choked. "Why didn't you tell me? Why?''

"There were so many things I didn't tell you. Because we never talked. Not about losing her. Not about the way we went on after.''

"We talked, Alice. We—''

She shook her head. "A few awkward exchanges, a mumbled word or two.''

He cupped her face once more. "What do you want me to say now, Alice? I'd like to give you what you need, but I don't know what it is. I don't know how.''

Her breath caught on a sob; she forced it back. And that was the crux of the problem. It was the reason their relationship would never work.

This was goodbye. Again.

Only this time, she let him go willingly.

She eased regretfully away from him. Tears slid down her cheeks. "I love you, Hayes. I don't think I ever stopped. I know now that loving you is why I didn't marry Stephen. I'd never gotten over you."

She brushed at her cheeks, at the tears. "But it's time. Loving you isn't enough anymore. I do want a family. A husband and children. And it's not too late for me." She looked him straight in the eye, even though hers were filled with tears. "You were right, Hayes. You are the wrong man for me. You won't make me happy. I see that now."

Hayes flinched, her words slicing through him like a dull, ragged blade, ripping, tearing. He drew in a deep breath. *How would he go on without her?*

He tightened his jaw, even as he acknowledged the ache that would never leave him. "I don't know what to say."

"Unless you can tell me you love me, there is nothing to say."

He fisted his fingers. Against the emotion charging through him, against the urge to tumble her into his arms and never let her go. The urge to fight for her. He had no right; he couldn't give her what she needed.

"Then go," he said, his voice thick. "We're not doing either of us any good standing here."

She hesitated one moment and his chest tightened with unreasonable hope. Then, eyes brimming with tears, she turned and walked toward Sheri's room. She stopped when she reached the door and looked back at him. "It's too bad, Hayes. We could have had something really great together. If only you had a heart."

Hayes watched as she tapped lightly on Sheri's door, then disappeared inside, the door snapping shut behind her. Snapping shut on their relationship.

He brought the heels of his hands to his eyes. She'd told him everything he'd already known. He wouldn't make her happy; he was the wrong man for her.

So why did he hurt so bad? Why did watching her walk away feel so wrong?

Jeff emerged from Sheri's room, his head bent and shoulders hunched. He paused outside the door, then crossed to where Hayes stood, stopping in front of him, fists and jaw clenched, spoiling for a fight.

"Well, you got what you wanted," Jeff said, his voice choked with emotion. "You win."

Hayes met his gaze evenly, although it hurt to do so. "This isn't what I wanted. And I'm terribly sorry. I know how much you must hurt."

"Right." Jeff took a step closer, a muscle working in his jaw, his eyes dark with emotion. "You never wanted this baby to be born. You don't care now that it's..." His throat closed over the words, and his eyes filled. "Don't pretend with me that you give a damn. Because I don't buy it."

"All I've ever wanted is the best for you. What I thought was the best, anyway." Hayes laid his hand on Jeff's shoulder. "And I never thought of it as a competition, son. Never."

"Bull!" Jeff knocked Hayes's hand away and brought his fists up. "It always had to be your way or no way. Not this time!"

Hayes narrowed his eyes, battling remorse, regrets so strong they stole his breath. "If it'll make you feel better, take a swing at me. But I warn you, you'll only take one."

Jeff drew his fist back and Hayes braced himself for the blow, then with a cry of pain Jeff dropped his fist and pushed past him. Hayes let him go. He understood his son's grief. His anger. He understood why Jeff had directed it at him. But understanding didn't make it any less painful.

For the second time tonight, heart breaking, he watched a piece of himself walk away.

A lump formed in his throat. He'd lost everything. Alice. Jeff. The grandchild he would never know.

Minutes ticked past. He didn't move. He stood in that sterile, uncomfortable waiting room, unable, or unwilling, to walk away. He had no reason not to leave. And every reason to stay.

Alice stepped out of Sheri's room. Her eyes met his; they were wet with tears. He longed to cross the hall and sweep her into his arms, longed to love and comfort her. He couldn't. Only minutes ago, he'd lost his right to touch her ever again.

Without speaking, she turned and walked away. The lump in his throat became a boulder; he shifted his gaze to Sheri's closed door. He swallowed, the reflexive action painful because of the emotion choking him. He crossed to Sheri's room, stopping in front of it.

Room E-eighteen. He frowned. Would that room number be burned into his memory as another one had been?

Seven-twenty.

Alice's room number twelve years ago.

He shifted his gaze from the room number to the doorknob. Almost without a will of his own, he reached for it, twisted and stepped inside.

Sheri slept. She lay on her back, her hands curved protectively over her abdomen even in sleep. Her skin was pale, as white as the sheets, her eyes shadowed.

He crossed to her side hesitantly. He felt like both an intruder and monumentally out of his depth. He stopped by the bed. Curling his hands around the rail, he gazed down at her.

Emotion rose up inside him in a debilitating wave, threatening to swallow him, drowning out everything rational and controllable, swamping him with memories and regrets and wishes for things that had never come to fruition. That never would.

To me, she was always little Margaret.

The child he had lost.

Why hadn't Alice told him that she'd named their child? He would have liked her to have a name, would have liked to have known it. It would have given him a modicum of peace.

Alice had thought he didn't care; she'd thought he hadn't grieved at the loss of their child.

He'd never stopped.

Tears stung his eyes, and horrified, he fought them back. Men didn't cry. Men were strong. Emotionally invincible. They conquered civilizations and board rooms, they erected cities and built armies.

But could they feel? Could they love? He'd loved their little one, their little...Margaret. Alice wouldn't believe that, he knew. She thought he had no heart, and he hadn't been able to find the words to tell her otherwise.

Why hadn't he been able to? Why hadn't he found a way to show her? He'd tried the only way he'd known how. By being strong for her. By not falling apart.

But that hadn't been enough. It never would be.

What good was love if it couldn't be expressed?

Hayes moved his gaze over Sheri's sleeping face. And what of Jeff? He cherished his son beyond words, would lay down his life for him. And yet, he'd done everything wrong. So wrong that now, when his son should need him most, he wouldn't allow him close, wouldn't allow even a word of comfort from him.

Sheri whimpered and stirred in her sleep, her face creasing with discomfort. Hayes reached out and touched her hair lightly. Tenderly. "I'm so sorry," he whispered. "You probably wouldn't believe me if you were awake. Jeff didn't. But it's—" His throat closed over the words and he cleared it. "It's true. I'm so terribly sorry."

She stirred again, and he drew his hand quickly away. "I . . . don't express my feelings very well. I feel so lost with them. So inept. But I do have feelings. I do care." He paused, grief swelling inside him. "I lost my grandchild tonight. And it . . . hurts."

His voice thickened; his eyes stung, and he shifted his gaze to the window. "I know what people call me. Bradford-the-cold-heart. If only that were true. Then I wouldn't be standing here feeling like I'd been ripped wide and left to bleed to death."

He returned his gaze to Sheri's face, touched her hair again, this time brushing it away from her cool forehead. "Alice and I lost a baby. A long time ago. Did you know that? Jeff never knew. We had decided to wait to tell him that Alice was expecting and then...

"I guess what I'm trying to say is, I understand what you and Jeff are going through. I know how much you both wanted this baby. Because...I really wanted my baby, the one that died." He brought his hands back to the bed rail, and curved his fingers around it. "And it...hurt so much when we lost her."

Hayes drew in a ragged breath. "It was never you, Sheri. I know you thought it was, but I didn't disapprove of you or think you weren't right for my son. I only thought he wasn't ready for marriage and a family. I thought he was too young.

"You're a brave girl, Sheri Kane. Braver than I am." He made a small sound of self-derision. "And you probably wouldn't believe this either, but I'd be proud to have you for a daughter-in-law."

Sheri's eyes opened and met his. They were a clear blue, unclouded by sleep or sedatives, and for long moments they gazed at each other.

"I do believe you," she whispered, her voice weak with fatigue and despair. "And I think you...would have made a good father-in-law."

Hayes didn't know what to say. He gazed at the teenager, his eyes swimming. Something about her seemed years older and wiser than her seventeen years. She had a way about her that made him feel at once comforted and at a total loss.

She reached up and covered his hand with her own. He curved his fingers around her cold ones, holding hers gently. "Where's Jeff?"

His expression must have said it all, because her eyes filled. "Go after him. He was so...upset. He needs you."

Hayes shook his head, emotion choking him. "He doesn't . . . need me. He doesn't want my comfort."

She squeezed his fingers. "He does. He wants it . . . more than anything."

Her eyelids fluttered, and Hayes could see sleep pulling at her. He gazed at her face, her words running through his head. Did Jeff need him? If he reached out in the right way, would his son reach back?

Sheri could help him. She knew Jeff better than anyone, even himself.

He caught his breath. She *could* help him. She would know if he had a chance of salvaging his relationship with his son.

"Sheri?" She opened her eyes, and he leaned toward her. "Why is Jeff so angry with me? Tell me how to reach him. Tell me what I did wrong."

A weak smile pulled at her mouth. "It's not what you . . . did. It's what you didn't . . ."

Her eyelids fluttered again, her voice was smudged with fatigue. Hayes leaned closer. "What, Sheri? What didn't I do?"

She forced her eyes back open. "He thinks you . . . don't . . . love him."

Her eyes shut and her hand slackened in his. For long moments he continued to hold it, his head whirling with what she'd said, then he laid it softly by her side.

His son thought he didn't love him.

No wonder Jeff was so angry. No wonder he saw his father's every comment as a criticism, his every suggestion as a statement of dissatisfaction. The dilemma of Sheri's pregnancy had brought Jeff's feelings to a head because Jeff had been forced to state his mind and Hayes had been forced to disagree.

Guilt rushed over him. As did remorse. He racked his brain. When was the last time he'd said the words *I love you?* Had he ever?

A sick feeling settled in the pit of his stomach as he realized the truth. But he'd tried to show Jeff how he felt in other ways. By always being there for him. By teaching him right from wrong, by being strong.

It hadn't been enough. Not nearly.

Was it too late?

He had to find him. He had to talk to him. Leaning down, he pressed a kiss to Sheri's forehead. "Thank you," he whispered. "Thank you so very much."

Heart thundering, Hayes let himself out of Sheri's room, then left the hospital. Dawn had begun to replace the dark; the glimmer of light on the horizon announced the birth of a new day.

Hayes stood in the hospital parking lot and gazed at the sliver of light creeping over the horizon.

Jeff had gone to the bridge where his mother had died. Just as he had the night of the storm.

Hayes shook his head. What reason did he have to think that? Jeff had probably walked home. Or was waiting for him at the car. Lack of sleep had affected his judgment—the Madisonville Bridge was miles from there.

Even as he told himself he had no reason to think Jeff had gone anywhere but home, he knew he was right. His gut told him. And his heart.

Hayes found his car and climbed inside. Ignoring logic, he headed for Madisonville, taking the back roads, thinking he might find Jeff at the side of one, walking.

By the time he'd reach the bridge, dawn had eased completely over the horizon, shooting the sky with spears of brilliant color. Relief rolled over him in a sweet, dizzying wave as he saw that his hunch had been right. Jeff stood at the center of the old bridge, hands at his sides, eyes on the water.

He hadn't realized until that moment that he'd been afraid for Jeff. Afraid he would do something stupid and desperate.

Hayes stopped the car and climbed out, closing the door softly behind him. Even so the sound echoed on the still morning air. Praying for the right words, he started up the bridge.

Jeff never glanced his way, never took his gaze from the water. He looked so young, Hayes thought, a catch in his chest. Too young to have had to face what he had tonight. Too young to be so alone.

Hayes stopped beside him and, not speaking, turned his own gaze to the water.

"How did you know I was here?"

Hayes turned and met his son's eyes. He saw that they were red from crying. His heart turned over. "I just knew."

"Great." Jeff let out a bitter, defeated breath. "You won again. Now, just go away."

"No." Hayes shook his head. "I'm not going to do that. I can't. We need to talk."

Jeff's eyes welled with tears, and he jerked his gaze away, obviously embarrassed by the emotion.

He'd taught him that, Hayes realized. Taught him to be embarrassed by emotion. Taught him to be uncomfortable with it. Just as his father had taught him. He'd made so many mistakes.

Tonight he would take the first step toward righting them.

"You lost your baby, Jeff. It's okay to hurt. It's okay to cry. It doesn't make you less of a man."

"No?" Jeff turned his head away, brushing at his cheeks. "When have you ever cried? When have you ever hurt?"

"Tonight. For you and Sheri. For myself." He thought of Alice, and his chest tightened almost unbearably. "I still hurt."

Jeff stood absolutely still, and although his son didn't look at him, Hayes knew he had his attention. "I can understand why that's hard for you to believe. I've been wrong about so many things. About how a man should live. About what other people needed from me." He jammed his hands into his sweatshirt pockets. "About what I needed."

Jeff turned toward him, his face twisted with pain. "You never needed anything. You were always so...in control. So fearless. I tried to be like you, but I...I always fell short."

He'd never had any idea Jeff felt that way. He'd never had a clue. He shook his head. "For God's sake, son, don't try to be like me. I've been scared witless for so long that until tonight I didn't know what was real anymore. I do now."

At his son's shocked expression, Hayes laughed, the sound tight and humorless. "After your mother died, I blamed myself. For her unhappiness. Her death. I was so busy placing blame I didn't have time to feel how much her leaving hurt me. I always thought in terms of how much she hurt *you*." Hayes drew is eye-brows together. "But I hurt, too. So much, the idea of loving someone again scared me to death."

Hayes squeezed his hands into fists, thinking of all the things he wished he could change and telling himself the only way to change them was to go forward. To shape the future.

His and Jeff's future.

He met his son's gaze. "I always needed you, Jeff. I always loved you." As he said the words, a dam broke inside him, spilling out warmth. And light. "I don't know why I couldn't say it before. I always thought it. And I always felt it. These past months, I've been terrified that it was too late for us, terrified that I'd driven you away. You're my son, and I don't know what I would do if I lost you."

Hayes took a deep breath. "Have I lost you, Jeff? Is it too late for us to start being father and son, the way it should be? Could we try?"

For long moments Jeff stood, head lowered, unmoving. Then he lifted his eyes to his father's. The joy in them took Hayes's breath away.

"I'd like that, Dad."

It was going to be all right. He hadn't lost his son. Thank God.

Hayes hugged Jeff tightly. Jeff hugged him back. For long moments after, they stared out at the water, shimmering golden with the new day, lost in their own thoughts. After a time, Jeff turned to him, sorrow in his eyes.

"I know you didn't think I was ready, but I really wanted the baby. I don't know how, but it just became a part of me so fast." Jeff drew in a ragged breath and tilted his face to the delicately painted sky. "It hurts. Really bad."

Hayes swallowed, the helpless feeling he'd always abhorred washing over him. But instead of feeling as if he were losing something, he realized he'd found something instead. The ability to feel. To be a whole person, frailties and all.

A person who could love. Openly. And one who could hurt, too.

Alice.

Hayes caught his breath. He loved her. He had all along. And all along he'd been terrified of being hurt.

He would make her happy. They would make each other happy.

The truth barreled through him, freeing him. He had to find her. And convince her. He prayed he wasn't too late, that he hadn't mucked things up so badly she wouldn't look at him, let alone give him another chance.

Jeff turned his anguished eyes on Hayes. "Tell me how to make the pain go away. I don't know how."

Hayes hugged his son again. Hard. "Time," he said softly. "And love. Lots and lots of love."

Chapter Thirteen

The house hadn't changed. Small and squalid, it occupied the middle lot on a rundown street in the worst part of Covington. Even the trees that lined the street looked beaten and sad. Alice shut off her car's engine, but didn't make a move to get out. She gazed at the structure's sagging front porch, its cracked and peeling paint, and thought of her own neat cottage, with its bright white walls and freshly painted shutters.

She'd come a long way.

Or had she? She looked down at her hands, curved so tightly around the steering wheel her knuckles were white, tuned in to her out-of-control heartbeat. She lived in a nice neighborhood now, in a lovely home; she had a good education, a good job.

Yet she wasn't so far removed from the frightened little girl who had hidden from her mother in a broom closet.

Hiding.

She'd been doing a lot of that. Hiding and running. Hayes had accused her of both, and although she hated to admit it was true . . . it was.

As she thought of Hayes, tears welled in her eyes. She fought them off. Not because she wanted to avoid her own feelings, but because, since walking away from him five hours ago, she'd cried enough to last a lifetime.

Lord, she loved him.

But she wouldn't look back. Today, this moment, she would move forward with her life.

Alice forced herself to let go of the wheel and open the car door. She took a deep breath and stepped out. She couldn't run from her past any longer. She couldn't hide from her mother.

The house may not have changed.

But she had. She'd grown up.

Alice slammed the car door and started up the walk. The front steps dipped as she stepped on them; the porch floor creaked and groaned. She knocked on the door, not even able to hear the sound of her own knuckles for the wild pounding of her heart.

Seconds ticked past. From inside she heard the sound of someone stumbling around. Ten a.m. was early for an alcoholic, Alice thought, a sick feeling in the pit of her stomach. Especially for one who liked to binge at night.

How could she have forgotten that? From the time she was old enough to remember, she'd gotten her own breakfast, had gotten herself washed and dressed and off to school. Her parents had never been up before afternoon.

The door swung open; her mother stood on the other side, gazing at her with narrowed eyes. Alice's heart flew to her throat. She could make herself all manner of assurances about being an adult, yet looking into her mother's lined face, she felt like a child.

A child who expected the back of a hand.

Alice's eyes skimmed over Marge Dougherty. Her mother's face had aged tremendously in the years since Alice had seen her last. It was a face marked by every drink, every cigarette, every unkind and bitter thought. Her hair was grayer than Alice remembered; she wore an ancient housecoat and an unlit cigarette dangled from between her lips.

"Yeah?" she asked, lighting the cigarette with a hand that shook badly. "What do you want? It's early."

Her mother didn't recognize her.

She could apologize, Alice realized. Make up some story about having the wrong address and escape. But if she did, she would never know the truth.

And she would never be free of her past.

She stiffened her spine. "It's me. Alice."

"Alice?" Her mother squinted against the haze of smoke. "Son of a...it is you. My little baby, all grown up."

Her little baby? She hadn't been that in a long time. If ever. A knot of denial in her stomach, Alice hiked her purse strap higher on her shoulder. "May I come in?"

"Yeah, sure." She swung the door wider. "Make yourself at home."

At home. Alice followed her inside, gooseflesh sliding up her arms. *This place had never been her home, even when she'd lived here.*

She moved her gaze hesitantly around the room, looking for something, waiting for something, although she wasn't sure what.

Her father, maybe? A feeling of dread? The ghosts of her unhappy childhood?

She took in the battered furniture, the coffee table littered with beer bottles, overflowing ashtrays and take-out bags. Nothing happened. No boogeyman jumped out to get her. It was just a room, shabby and unkempt. Nothing more.

No one could hurt her unless she allowed it.

Alice sat on the edge of the couch and returned her gaze to her mother. "You've been trying to reach me. Why?"

"Why?" Her mother arched her eyebrows. "Like I told you in my letters, I wanted to get together with my little girl. We've been apart too long."

"I mean, why now?" Alice clasped her hands in her lap. "Why now, after all these years?"

Her mother drew deeply on her cigarette, coughing as she exhaled. "I'm all alone now, and I thought that being family and all, we should be together."

Together. That's the way she'd always heard families should be. It's what she'd always dreamed of. But her mother didn't even know her. She'd tossed her away years ago.

Alice tightened her fingers in her lap. "What you're saying is, now that you're alone, you want to be a part of my life?"

"Yeah." Her mother narrowed her eyes, and snubbed out the cigarette. "That's what I said. We should be together. I'm your mama, after all."

Mama. Alice thought of Sheri and of what she'd been through, of how much she'd loved and worried about her unborn child, and tears pricked at her eyes.

In the months Sheri had carried her baby, the young woman had been a better mother than Alice's had been in all the years they'd been together.

Alice met her mother's eyes. As she did, she saw her mother for what she was—a woman who had had a hard life, but one who had never had the strength of character, or the desire, to better herself. A woman who had never cared for anyone or anything but herself. A person who was selfish and unkind. But not a monster. Not a larger-than-life being with the power to destroy her daughter.

Alice had given her that power.

As the truth of that began sinking in, layers of her childhood fears and pain began to fall away from her. Leaving her whole and strong. Unafraid.

She didn't need her mother's love or approval, she realized. Her mother was incapable of loving her. And that was okay. She loved herself. She approved of herself. She didn't need to be validated by her mother or anyone else.

She'd finally said goodbye to her past.

Alice stood. "I'm sorry, but it won't be possible for us to spend time together. Any relationship we had ended a long time ago."

"What?" Her mother's face slackened, then tightened in fury. "Family should take care of each other. That's the way it's supposed to be."

Alice sucked in a sharp breath, anger blooming inside her. Outrage that after everything her mother had done—and not done—she could sit there and spout words about family and responsibility. She fisted her fingers. "You know nothing about the way it's supposed to be. Being a family is about loving. About cherishing and protecting and sharing. Now that you're alone, you want me to take care of you. Where were you when I was five? When I was ten and fourteen?" She shook her head. "We're not family. We never have been."

"You . . . can't do this," Marge sputtered. "It's not right." She followed Alice to her feet. "What kind of daughter are you? Abandoning your old mama when she needs you most? What kind—"

Alice stopped her. "I forgive you for how you treated me. As much as I can, considering I'm human. I give you the benefit of the doubt and believe that you didn't know any better, that your mother probably treated you just as badly as you treated me." She started for the door, stopping and turning back to her mother when she reached it. She met her mother's gaze evenly. "I won't let you back into my life."

"I gave you life!" her mother shrieked. "You owe me."

Alice shook her head and opened the door. "I came here today because I believe people can change. And I believe everyone deserves a second chance. But you haven't changed and you don't want to. I don't owe you anything. I owed it to myself to face you one last time, and I did. You should be glad for me, glad that I broke the ugly cycle.'' She stepped through the door. ''Please don't contact me again. Goodbye... Marge.''

Alice shut the door, then drew in a deep, cleansing breath. The day tasted sweet and pure, the sunshine spilled over her, bright and healing.

She smiled. She *didn't* need her mother's love or approval anymore. She didn't need anyone's. She knew who she was, and she liked that person a lot.

She drew in another breath. She was no longer a needy and vulnerable little girl, hungry for love but certain of rejection.

She flew down the porch steps and to her car, feeling free for the first time in her life. Of the past and her fears. Of a need that had always left her feeling empty and less-than.

She opened her car door and slipped inside. Catching a glimpse of herself in the rearview mirror, she smiled. Then laughed. The past didn't matter. The girl she'd been didn't matter. She loved herself.

Hayes.

She'd expected something of him she hadn't been able to give herself. Trust. Emotional honesty. The courage to love no matter the outcome or consequences.

She'd been so sure he was going to reject her she hadn't given their relationship a real chance.

She shook her head. He wouldn't make her happy? He *did* make her happy. And he was as scared of being hurt as she had been.

He loved her.

And if he didn't, he should. She laughed again and started the car. She would prove it to him.

Pulling away from the curb, she left her past behind forever. And went in search of Hayes. And her future.

Hayes was nowhere to be found. Alice flexed her fingers on the steering wheel in frustration and turned onto her narrow street. She had tried his office, the hospital; she'd sat on his front steps waiting for him for nearly four hours. Where could he be?

On her own front porch.

She stopped her car in the middle of the street, forcing the driver behind her to slam on his brakes and earning the blare of his horn and shouted epithet.

Hayes looked up. Her heart turned over. Judging by the assortment of take-out bags beside him, all from the seafood joint down the street, he'd been sitting there a long time.

Waiting for her.

He loved her.

She squeezed her eyes shut. It had to be true. Why else would he be here, waiting for her?

The driver behind her honked again, and she started the car and maneuvered it into the space in front of her cottage, trembling so badly it took her three tries to get it right. Heart thundering, she turned off the engine and alighted from the car.

Hayes's eyes never left hers. He stood and watched her as she crossed to him, unmoving, his expression guarded.

She stopped at the bottom of the stairs and tilted her face up to his. In his eyes she saw something she never had before, but something she'd always longed to see. Hope blossomed inside her. "Hello, Hayes."

He slipped his hands into his pockets. "Hi."

She motioned toward the bags. "Looks like you've been waiting awhile."

"You could say that."

And she'd been waiting all her life. For this moment. For him. She took another step, then another, stopping when they stood face-to-face. She tilted her face up to his. "At the hospital I told you that unless you could tell me you loved me, we had nothing to say to each other." She took a deep breath and said a silent prayer. "Do we have anything to say to each other, Hayes?"

He searched her gaze, his expression solemn. Then, without warning, he tumbled her into his arms. "God, yes. I love you . . . I love you . . . I love—"

She brought his mouth down to hers. Their mouths met and clung; they held on to each other tightly, afraid that if they let go the other would disappear.

After a time, Hayes drew away and cupped her face in his hands, touching her almost reverently. "I was so afraid of being hurt again, the way I was with Isabel, that I tried to keep you at arm's length. I told myself I was protecting you. I told myself that I would make you unhappy, that I would hurt you. But the truth is, I was protecting myself. I was certain *I* would be hurt. I couldn't see that I loved you until tonight, when I almost lost you and everyone else in my life."

She smiled. "I was wrong, too, Hayes. I expected you to be someone you're not. Even though you're the man I love. Even though I love everything about you. Your strength and loyalty. The logical way you look at

the world. The way you can express your feelings
without ever saying a word.''

She touched his mouth with her fingertip. "The way
you're doing right now. You're the right man for me,
Hayes Bradford. You always will be."

"I'll make you happy, Alice. I promise I will."

She trailed a finger across his lips. "No," she cor-
rected. "We'll make each other happy. That's the way
it's supposed to be."

He kissed her again, this time taking her fully into
his arms, possessing her mouth completely. A car full
of teenagers drove by, and the rowdy kids honked and
shouted. One of them recognized her and called her
name.

Alice pulled back, her cheeks heating. "By noon
Monday it'll be all over Hope House that I was neck-
ing on my front porch."

He laughed softly. "We should have met on my
front porch. It's more private."

"I tried that." At his look, she laughed and slid her
hands around his neck. "While you were waiting here,
I was on your front porch."

"While I was here?"

"Mmm-hmm." She leaned against him. "To the
tune of about four hours. Before that, I went to see my
mother."

Hayes drew his eyebrows together. "But I called
Maggie. She said she hadn't seen you."

"Not Maggie." She stood on tiptoes and kissed him,
a smile tugging at her mouth. "My biological mother.
But that's another story. I'll tell you all about it.
Soon."

"But not now?"

"Uh-uh." She laced their fingers. "Now I have other plans."

With a soft laugh, Hayes let her lead him inside.

Epilogue

"Just how big is that bird, Alice?" Hayes eyed the turkey as she maneuvered it out of the grocery bag. "And are you even sure it's a turkey? It looks more like a small horse."

"Very funny." She arched an eyebrow indignantly at her husband. "A twenty-six-pound turkey is not that big. Especially considering Maggie and her brood are coming. Josh alone will pack away a third of the bird."

Hayes laughed. "Oh, sure. Blame it on Josh. Are you telling me that the size of that bird doesn't have anything to do with the fact that you're eating for three now?"

Alice placed a hand on her swollen belly, a soft smile tugging at her mouth. *Twins. Perfectly healthy and thriving. She still couldn't believe it.* "Are you calling me a glutton, Counselor?"

He tumbled her into his arms and kissed her soundly. Lifting his head, he grinned. "I plead the Fifth."

She tipped her head toward Sheri. The teenager stood anxiously at the window, looking out. Jeff was due home any minute, his first trip back since leaving for Georgetown, and Sheri hadn't budged from the window all morning. "What do you think? Should I show him mercy? Or throw the book at him?"

The teenager dragged her gaze from the window, her eyebrows drawn with worry. "I'm sorry, what did you say?"

Alice's heart tipped over, and she shot the girl a sympathetic smile. "Never mind. It was just silliness."

Hayes kissed her again, then released her. "I'll get the rest of the groceries."

"Thanks." As he started past her, she caught his hand. He stopped and met her eyes. She smiled. "I love you."

He brought her hand to his mouth. "I love you, too."

Hayes headed out the back door, and Alice crossed to Sheri. She laid a hand on the girl's shoulder. "He'll be here. Don't worry."

"That's not what I'm worrying about." Sheri caught her bottom lip between her teeth and glanced over her shoulder at Alice. "Do you think it'll be, you know, the same between us?"

"Goose." She tapped the end of Sheri's nose. "He writes you every week and your phone bill rivals the national debt. Of course it will."

For long moments the teenager gazed out the window, before turning to Alice once more. "But what if . . . college has changed him? Or changed the way he looks at me?" She clasped her hands together. "What if, after being around all those college girls, he doesn't love me anymore?"

"Never."

Alice and Sheri swung simultaneously toward the kitchen doorway. Jeff stood there, arms loaded with grocery bags, his face wreathed in a smile, his eyes only for Sheri. Hayes stood beside him, looking every inch the proud and happy father.

"Never," Jeff repeated, handing Hayes the bags and opening his arms. Sheri ran to them.

As the teenagers embraced, Hayes shifted his gaze to Alice. Her heart turned over at the wealth of emotion in his eyes.

A family. They were a family at last.

* * * * *

Dark secrets, dangerous desire...

Lovers DARK AND DANGEROUS

Three spine-tingling tales from the dark side of love.

This October, enter the world of shadowy romance as Silhouette presents the third in their annual tradition of thrilling love stories and chilling story lines. Written by three of Silhouette's top names:

LINDSAY McKENNA
LEE KARR
RACHEL LEE

Haunting a store near you this October.

Only from

Silhouette®

...where passion lives.

Silhouette Books
is proud to present
our best authors, their best books...
and the best in your reading pleasure!

Throughout 1994, look for exciting books
by these top names in contemporary
romance:

DIANA PALMER
Enamored in August

HEATHER GRAHAM POZZESSERE
The Game of Love in August

FERN MICHAELS
Beyond Tomorrow in August

NORA ROBERTS
The Last Honest Woman in September

LINDA LAEL MILLER
Snowflakes on the Sea in September

*When it comes to passion,
we wrote the book.*

BOBQ3

THE PARSON'S WAITING
Sherryl Woods

A life of harsh assignments had hardened
correspondent Richard Walton. Yet his heart yearned
for tenderness and warmth. He'd long ago given up
the search for these precious qualities—until town
parson Anna Louise Perkins entered his life. This
courageous, loving woman's presence could be the
cure Richard's soul so desperately sought....

Maddening men...winsome women...and the untamed land
they live in—all add up to love!

A RIVER TO CROSS (SE #910)
Laurie Paige

Sheriff Shane Macklin knew there was more to "town outsider"
Tina Henderson than met the eye. What he saw was a generous
and selfless woman whose true colors held the promise of love....

Don't miss the latest Rogue River tale, A RIVER TO CROSS, available
in September from Silhouette Special Edition!

BABY'S CHOICE

Those mischievous matchmaking babies are back, as Marie Ferrarella's Baby's Choice series continues in August with MOTHER ON THE WING (SR #1026).

Frank Harrigan could hardly explain his sudden desire to fly to Seattle. Sure, an old friend had written to him out of the blue, but there was something else.... Then he spotted Donna McCollough, or rather, she fell right into his lap. And from that moment on, they were powerless to interfere with what angelic fate had lovingly ordained.

Continue to share in the wonder of life and love, as babies-in-waiting handpick the most perfect parents, only in

Silhouette

R O M A N C E™

To order your copy of the first Baby's Choice title, *Caution: Baby Ahead* (SR #1007), please send your name, address, zip or postal code, along with a check or money order (please do not send cash) for $2.75, plus 75¢ postage and handling ($1.00 in Canada), payable to Silhouette Books, to:

In the U.S.	In Canada
Silhouette Books	Silhouette Books
3010 Walden Ave.	P. O. Box 636
P. O. Box 9077	Fort Erie, Ontario
Buffalo, NY 14269-9077	L2A 5X3

Please specify book title with your order.
Canadian residents add applicable federal and provincial taxes.

SRMF2

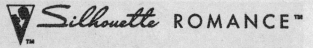
Silhouette ROMANCE™

First comes marriage.... Will love follow?
Find out this September when Silhouette Romance presents

Join six couples who marry for convenient reasons, and still find happily-ever-afters. Look for these wonderful books by some of your favorite authors:

#1030 *Timely Matrimony* by Kasey Michaels
#1031 *McCullough's Bride* by Anne Peters
#1032 *One of a Kind Marriage* by Cathie Linz
#1033 *Oh, Baby!* by Lauryn Chandler
#1034 *Temporary Groom* by Jayne Addison
#1035 *Wife in Name Only* by Carolyn Zane

by Christine Rimmer

Three rapscallion brothers. Their main talent: making trouble. Their only hope: three uncommon women who knew the way to heal a wounded heart! Meet them in these books:

Jared Jones

hadn't had it easy with women. Retreating to his mountain cabin, he found willful Eden Parker waiting to show him a good woman's love in MAN OF THE MOUNTAIN (May, SE #886).

Patrick Jones

was determined to show Regina Black that a wild Jones boy was *not* husband material. But that wouldn't stop her from trying to nab him in SWEETBRIAR SUMMIT (July, SE #896)!

Jack Roper

came to town looking for the wayward and beautiful Olivia Larrabee. He never suspected he'd uncover a long-buried Jones family secret in A HOME FOR THE HUNTER (September, SE #908)....

Meet these rascal men and the women who'll tame them, only from Silhouette Books and Special Edition!

If you missed either of the first two books in THE JONES GANG series, *Man of the Mountain* (SE #886), or *Sweetbriar Summit* (SE #896), order your copy now by sending your name, address, zip or postal code along with a check or money order (please do not send cash) for $3.50 ($3.99 in Canada for SE #896) plus 75¢ postage and handling ($1.00 in Canada), payable to Silhouette Books, to:

In the U.S.	In Canada
Silhouette Books	Silhouette Books
3010 Walden Ave.	P. O. Box 636
P. O. Box 9077	Fort Erie, Ontario
Buffalo, NY 14269-9077	L2A 5X3

Please specify book title(s) with order.
Canadian residents add applicable federal and provincial taxes.